At that moment, Ryan noticed something strange. For the most part, wherever he pointed the flashlight, the beam of light bounced off the tree trunks and away into the distance. But at one place, it was different. Just to his left, the light seemed to hit some kind of object: a shiny object, which reflected the light back into his eyes.

Cautiously, Ryan stretched out his arm and reached as far as the thorns and creepers would allow – fearful that, at any minute, a wolf might leap up and sink its fangs into his hand.

There was no wolf. Yet, when Ryan made contact with what was there, his blood turned icy in his veins.

The object was cold, hard and smooth to the touch. He knew what it must be. It felt like the black marble clock tower of his nightmare. Had he really found the Clock of Doom?

CLOCK OF DOOM

Paul Stewart

ISBN 0 7460 2474 6 (paperback)
ISBN 0 7460 2475 4 (hardback)

U.E. First Published in America March 1997

Typeset in Palatino
Printed in Great Britain

Series Editor: Gaby Waters
Editor: Phil Roxbee Cox
Designer: Lucy Parris
Cover illustration: Barry Jones

CONTENTS

1

Greetings

Ryan Schilling stepped down onto the deserted platform of Steinfeld Station. It was bitterly cold after the warmth of the compartment. When he breathed in, the freezing air hurt his nose and lungs. When he breathed out, thick coils of mist wrapped themselves around his head. There wasn't a soul in sight.

His Uncle Karl had said he'd be there to meet him at the station. So where was he?

Ryan picked up his backpack and headed for the empty ticket barrier, hoping to find someone outside. He hadn't gone more than half a dozen steps when a huge dog skidded into view. It looked up, sniffed the air and, barking furiously, came hurtling across the platform at him.

Ryan froze. He wasn't a fan of strange dogs at the best of times, and this one was a *monster*. It was big and obviously strong, with a thick white coat and cold black eyes. As it got closer it bared its slobbering jaws. Ryan found himself staring at two rows of glistening razor-sharp teeth.

"Oh, what?" he groaned. Not two minutes off the train and already he'd come face to face with the hound from hell.

Ryan backed away, his heart racing. The dog launched itself into midair, its outstretched claws lunging up at him. He raised his backpack protectively and rammed it between the creature's gaping jaws.

As its teeth sank into the bag, the dog's paws thumped against Ryan's chest and sent him flying through the air. He landed with a heavy bump – at the very edge of the platform.

He looked up at the dog standing over him. Now that it had caught him, it seemed in no particular hurry to finish Ryan off.

"Gooood doggy!" Ryan cooed optimistically.

He saw the dog's ears prick up, and it turned and looked around. Then Ryan heard it too – the sound of footsteps echoing from the ticket hall, followed by a man's voice.

"Max!" it roared. "Heel, boy!"

The owner, thought Ryan. At last. But, ignoring the man's yells, the dog lowered its head. The vicious jaws parted. Ryan closed his eyes.

He felt warm breath on his face and with it the stench of rotten meat.

"MAX!" the man bellowed, and Ryan heard him racing across the platform.

Ryan flinched as the dog's wet, warm, and very rough tongue lapped at his chin, and up over his nose. He was being *tasted*.

The next instant, there was an abrupt jolt, and the weight on his chest disappeared.

"Ryan?" he heard. "It is you, isn't it?"

Ryan looked up. Standing there was a tall man with straw-like hair and bright blue eyes. Ryan recognized him from numerous snapshots. It was Uncle Karl – but, unlike his smiling pictures, this real Uncle Karl had a concerned look on his face.

"I'm so sorry about that," he said, helping Ryan to his feet. "Max doesn't usually behave this way. He must have been very excited about meeting you."

Ryan looked at the dog. With its wagging tail and lolling tongue, it – *he* – looked friendly now. All the same, Ryan was glad that his uncle had a firm hold on his collar.

Three days earlier it had been Ryan's birthday. Months before, his parents had promised him an extra special birthday present. He was to stay with

3

his Uncle Karl and Aunt Ingrid.

Ryan had been looking forward to the trip for ages. Most importantly, he would be visiting the country where his dad had grown up, and meeting his dad's brother face-to-face for the first time. It would also give him a chance to use his German, and maybe even learn to ski.

The journey had been an exciting one; all the more so for going by himself. The plane flight, the train ride, everything had gone without a hitch. And now here he was, only a car ride from Oberdorf where Uncle Karl and Aunt Ingrid lived, in the house where his dad had been born.

"I apologize for not being here on time," said his uncle. "The weather's suddenly turned. It's snowing heavily up in the mountains and the drive down here took longer than I expected."

Ryan was pleased to discover that understanding his uncle's German was no problem. Ryan looked up at the sky. It was a curdled yellow-grey.

"It's strange," said Uncle Karl, picking up Ryan's backpack. "There was no mention of bad weather on the TV this morning, and our weather forecasts are usually pretty accurate. The snow clouds just seemed to come from nowhere... probably about the time you crossed the border."

They began walking to the station exit, with Max straining at the leash.

"We'd better get a move on," said his uncle as they crossed the car park together. "It'll be snowing down here soon, and it's going to get a lot worse higher up the mountain."

"The way dad talks, it's *always* snowing in Oberdorf," said Ryan.

His uncle smiled. "Your dad exaggerates. There's always some snow in the mountains in the winter, but that doesn't mean it snows all the time... and we usually get some warning." They reached a large four-wheel drive vehicle. It was the only car in the car park.

Uncle Karl clapped his hand on his nephew's shoulder. "It's good to meet you at last, Ryan," he said. "Your Aunt Ingrid is very excited about your visit too. Let's get home."

They pulled out of the car park just as the first snow began to fall on the town of Steinfeld.

2

Storm brewing

By the time they'd reached the outskirts of town, it was impossible to see where the edge of the road was. Uncle Karl pulled the car over to one side. "I'll have to put the snowchains on," he said. "I don't think we'll make it without them, even with four-wheel drive."

Ryan peered up out of the passenger window and watched the grey and yellow clouds swirling dizzily across the sky.

"I can't understand it," Uncle Karl said, climbing back into the driver's seat and starting the engine. "Nothing like this showed up on the satellite pictures." They set off once more.

"Is this a *real* blizzard?" asked Ryan.

His uncle didn't answer immediately. His eyes fixed on the road ahead. "It could be. We do get them," he said, at last. "But some are worse than others. When I was your age, Oberdorf was cut off by snow for almost two weeks and, eighty years ago or so, eighteen people died when –"

"But that couldn't happen now, could it?" said Ryan. "Not with helicopters and computers and things?"

"No," Uncle Karl shook his head thoughtfully. "At least, I certainly hope not. But nature can still catch us off guard."

He turned the car onto the road to Oberdorf. The wipers had to struggle hard against the snow driving straight at them. It was getting thicker and thicker by the minute.

Ryan stared out of the side window. "I never realized snow could be so dangerous," he said.

"Five people died up on the glacier last year," said Uncle Karl. "They were skiing off-piste on a clear day when they were suddenly hit by an avalanche. But there won't be any skiing in this weather. The lifts won't be running..." He paused. "I've never seen the snow so thick on this stretch of road before."

Slowly, blindly, they made their way up the narrow road which snaked its way through the trees, hairpin bend after hairpin bend, up the mountainside. Ryan found himself gripping the seat. He peered out of the passenger window. Through the giddy, swirling mass of snow and beyond the white edges of the road was a sheer drop that fell away to nothing. Ryan could hear his heart beating out loud.

He glanced at his uncle who was hunched over the wheel with a frown of concentration on his face. "How far is Oberdorf now?" Ryan asked nervously.

"It should only take ten minutes from here," said Uncle Karl. "Though heaven knows how long we'll be in this."

Ryan looked through the side window again. Black tree trunks, white snow; the whole landscape had turned to monochrome. As they rounded one particularly sharp bend they saw a van parked up ahead. A man was on all fours struggling with snowchains on the wheels. Uncle Karl had to steer his way carefully around the van, taking the car perilously near the edge.

Suddenly, Ryan felt the car lose control. His stomach lurched and he could imagine all four wheels spinning powerlessly. He closed his eyes. They were sliding sideways – closer and closer to the sheer drop over the edge of the road.

Uncle Karl said nothing. The next instant, Ryan heard a reassuring crunch as the chains on the wheels gripped the surface. When he opened his eyes again, they had left the van well behind them.

They drove on in silence. The road curved and twisted its way up and up to the little mountain village of Oberdorf. The only sound was the rhythmic thud of the snowchains biting into the drifting snow.

It was darker now and Uncle Karl switched the headlights to full beam. Ryan stared ahead, mesmerized by the glittering snow which danced in the broad wedges of light. It looked like a vast swarm of white bees.

The road began to flatten out and Ryan was glad to see trees on both sides of the road. In the distance, he could just make out the shapes of rooftops and chimneys and a glimmer of light. Without warning Uncle Karl turned left, off the road and up a steep narrow track through the trees – a track that Ryan hadn't even noticed was there.

The car crept on at a snail's pace until they reached a clearing where the track ended. Through the snow, Ryan saw a wooden house with a steep, tiled roof. He recognized it at once. This was the house his dad had told him so much about – the house on the edge of a tall, dark forest. Right now it was impossible to make out the trees in the forest, or anything else for that matter. The snow was deep all around and in places it had drifted almost up to the windows.

"Here at last," said Uncle Karl with a sigh of relief. "And I'm not going out again tonight... not for anything!"

Ryan stepped out of the car, into thick, deep snow that came up to his knees. The cold hit him with a blast as a sudden gust of wind caught the car door and seized it from his grasp. The snowflakes seemed to whip themselves into a frenzied flurry, lashing at his body and stinging his face.

The windows of the house gave off a warm glow. Ryan noticed that someone had cleared the drifting snow from the front door, but it was already starting to build up again.

The door opened and a woman stood framed in light. Ryan didn't recognize her at first. In real life Aunt Ingrid looked softer and plumper than she did in photographs. And right now she was also looking worried. Ryan waded through the snow toward his aunt.

"Come in! Come in!" Aunt Ingrid called out in slightly accented English. "What weather we are having to greet you, Ryan."

Max jumped down from the car into a heap of snow. He shook and sniffed the air. He seemed wary and was whimpering. "What's wrong, boy?" asked Uncle Karl, obviously surprised by the dog's antics. In the distance, a clock chimed. For a brief instant, despite the comforting smell of wood smoke and cooking coming through the open door, Ryan felt a sudden shiver of unease.

He watched as Max's fur bristled and his ears went flat. The dog raised his head and howled. The desperate cry seemed to hang in the air and was followed by an eerie, distant echo before it was swallowed up by the snow.

3

Cut off

It was liver dumplings for supper. Ryan's dad was always going on about liver dumplings and how much he'd liked them as a boy. Now, for the first time, Ryan could taste them for himself. He'd always thought that liver was bad enough – but with dumplings... *yuck*, disgusting.

They turned out to be delicious. As he finished his third bowlful, Ryan's eyelids began to grow heavy. The warmth of the large kitchen was almost enough to block out all thought of the terrible weather outside. He yawned. It had been a long and exciting day.

"Why don't you go up to bed, if you're tired?"

suggested his aunt.

"We've put you in the little room right at the top of the house. It was your father's. In fact, I think it's the same bed, though it must have had a new mattress since then!"

"Great," said Ryan.

Ryan's dad, Peter Schilling, was born in Oberdorf and lived there until he went abroad to work. It was there that he'd met Ryan's mother. That was twenty years ago. They married and, later, Ryan was born. Peter hadn't been back to Oberdorf in all that time.

Aunt Ingrid looked at Ryan. "You would like to phone your parents before going to bed, Ryan?" she asked in English, bustling him into the hall. "To let them know you arrived safely."

Ryan picked up the phone. It was dead.

"What is the matter?" asked Aunt Ingrid, taking the receiver from him. She tutted irritably. "Karl," she called out. "The lines must be down."

"It's the weather," said Uncle Karl, appearing from the kitchen. Ryan was suddenly aware of the wind rattling at the shutters and buffeting the doors. "A pylon must have come down. They'll fix it when it stops snowing."

"You can try the mobile," said Ryan's aunt. She left the room and returned with a mobile phone which she handed to Ryan.

That didn't work either.

"That's odd," said Uncle Karl. "I just charged the battery. Maybe it's the weather interfering with the signal. Still, it can't be helped. You'll just have to try again in the morning."

Ryan smiled. "Okay," he said. "Good night."

"Good night, Ryan," said his uncle and aunt. "Pleasant dreams!"

Ryan turned and looked back. "Thanks," he said, but – for a fleeting moment and for no obvious reason – the strange feeling of unease he'd felt outside returned. But everything was so *nice* here; so cozy. I'm just tired, he thought.

The bedroom was just as his father had described it. There was a low, sloping ceiling and, instead of curtains, closed shutters beyond the windows kept out the light. On the wall, a cuckoo clock ticked softly. Ryan undressed quickly, switched off the lamp and slid under a billowing white cotton quilt.

The wind continued to whistle and whine outside. Downstairs, Max howled again and again. It was only when he was finally silenced by one last, furious *"Quiet, Max!"* from Uncle Karl, that Ryan heard the other desperate cries. It was as if every dog in Oberdorf had been upset by something. Was it the weather? Or was there something else?

Ryan pulled the quilt around his ears to shut out the noise. He thought of his dad as a child, tucked up warm and snug in the same soft downy bed. His eyes closed and he drifted off, almost at once, into a deep, dark sleep. 'Pleasant dreams', they'd said, and a pleasant dream he had... to begin with.

As the night went on, however, the sound of the snowstorm filtered into Ryan's thoughts. Little by little, the dream turned into a nightmare.

4

The nightmare

*R*yan sat in an empty compartment of a train. *He was on his way to Steinfeld, on his way to Uncle Karl, on his way to the place where his father was born. He had to get off soon. Station after station went past, but the train didn't stop. The train couldn't stop.*

On and on it went, plunging ever deeper into a dense forest. Ryan looked out through a giddy swirl of snow, down at the sheer drop that fell away to nothing at the side of the track.

A moment later, he found himself in the corridor, lurching and bumping past endless empty compartments. Suddenly, a locked door loomed up in front of him. The front of the train. Red letters on a huge sign flashed on and off, pulsing out a message:

DRIVER
No Way Out

Ryan's head was filled with the sound of a rhythmic thump that seemed to grow faster and faster... a shrill squeal of metal as the wheels sped on. He fell. Arms flailing, he hurtled toward the door... and simply passed right through it into the driver's cab. It was empty. Huge letters flashed before his eyes:

No way out
NO DRIVER

Ryan looked for the brake but saw buttons instead. Red buttons, blue buttons, green buttons... but which button would stop the train?

The forest rushed past the window in a dark blur, stirred up with a frenzy of snow. He was hurtling down a never-ending tunnel. And all the while, the pine needles scratched and scraped at the window, and the cold snow stung his face.

"This is only a dream," Ryan told himself. But he couldn't wake up.

The train was gone. Ryan was in the forest. Afraid and alone. "This is only a dream. I must wake up. This is only a dream..." But he could feel the cold. He could hear the snow crunching beneath his feet. He could see his misty breath coiling in the shadowy moonlight... and he somehow knew that he was being hunted. All that mattered was escape.

Ryan stumbled blindly through the thick undergrowth. Pine needles slashed at his face, barbed thorns snagged his clothes and gnarled roots tripped him... but on he went. Then he heard the mournful sound of a howling dog, a howling wolf, a hundred howling wolves... No escape.

The forest grew thicker, as thick as a hedge. Down he went on hands and knees, crawling along. "Escape, you must escape. This is only a dream..."

All of a sudden he was in a clearing, thick with snow on the edge of a tall, dark forest. And straight ahead was a row of burning, yellow eyes.

He opened his mouth to scream, but no sound would come. He turned to run but his legs were stuck. The yellow eyes stared out of the darkness and grew before his eyes.

Suddenly, he was face-to-face with a single monstrous beast with a thick white coat and cold yellow eyes. Ryan backed away. The wolf launched itself into the air, its yellow fangs bared...

Ryan raised his arms as the hot, rotten breath hit him in the face and he fell back, flying through the air over a white pile of snow, back over the edge and down a sheer drop that fell away...

He landed on something cold and smooth and hard. He turned his head and looked up. He was sitting at the foot of a marble staircase that led all the way up the outside of a tall tower... a tower which pointed to the sky like a black marble finger. A bell tolled far above him.

It was a clock tower.

Then Ryan was halfway up a flight of spiral stairs, winding around the outside of the tower like a helter skelter... No escape.

Up and up he climbed without the slightest effort. The walls, as smooth as glass, reflected a second Ryan climbing up beside him. Up and up and up... Suddenly, the stairs came to a halt. He was facing a blank wall of marble. The wolves howled far below. No door. No escape. Above him, the top of the clock tower disappeared into the clouds.

"And no way to get up there," he found himself saying.

"Oh, yes there is," came a voice. His reflection was grinning at him.

"I'm dreaming," said Ryan. "This is a dream."

"Then wake up." His reflection was talking to him. "Are you coming in or not?" it demanded. It reached out with its hand.

Ryan stretched out his own hand... and was yanked abruptly through the solid marble wall, and into the tower where the staircase continued into the gloom.

Up he went, step after marble step. A pale, gloomy glow was coming in through narrow slits in the walls. "No escape," he panted. "No escape."

Now Ryan was in a dark passageway, so low and narrow he had to continue on his knees. It was so dark that he couldn't see a thing.

And the air.

There was no air.

It was getting harder and harder... to.... breathe...

He desperately felt his way around the smooth walls, hoping to find some kind of concealed doorway. But there was none. The cold, hard slabs all refused to budge.

No escape.

I'll have to go back. I must go back.

But he couldn't go back. There was no room to turn and, no matter where Ryan stretched his arms and legs, he struck the wall. It was a trap. It had been a trap all along... He was trapped inside a black marble coffin.

"Help," he cried out desperately.

"HELP?" boomed an unearthly voice. "YOU COME INSIDE THE TOWER WITHOUT PERMISSION," it cried. "AND NOW YOU ASK FOR HELP?"

"But I didn't know..."

"YOUR IGNORANCE IS OF NO CONCERN TO ME," the unearthly voice retorted. "YOU'RE HERE AND HERE YOU SHALL REMAIN."

Ryan clawed frantically at the walls. He must escape. He must...

... He must...

The unearthly voice was speaking again, so loud that the black marble itself vibrated.

"THERE'S NO ESCAPE... ESCAPE... ESCAPE...," it

bellowed, the words echoing away to nothing.

No escape.

"This is only a dream," Ryan kept on telling himself. "Only a dream."

5

Emergency!

Ryan woke up with a start. He opened his eyes and stifled a scream. He couldn't see, he couldn't move – he could scarcely even breathe. He was still trapped inside the black marble coffin...

Then he realized that the 'ceiling' just above him was soft and warm. It was only the quilt! He kicked it off.

His body wet with sweat, he lay still for a moment, breathing fast and shallow with relief. The nightmare was still vivid in his mind.

Ryan sat up in the bed. He'd had nightmares before but this was different. The events were still clear in his mind; every move, every sound... the train, the wolf, the tolling bell, the clock tower pointing to the sky like a black marble finger, and the unearthly voice.

Strangest of all, the fear he'd felt was still with him, lurking somehow just below the surface. He shivered. The memory of being walled up inside the clock tower was terrifyingly real.

He climbed out of bed, pulled on his clothes and padded across the room. He fumbled with the latch and pulled open the window. Then he tried to open the shutters. At first, they wouldn't budge. Then, with a swoosh-*flupp* the snow on the window ledge slipped down into the drift below, the shutters flew back, and the room was filled with dazzling sunshine.

He looked around. Everything was white, softly rounded, and twinkling in the bright sunlight. It was like looking down on clouds from an aircraft, without the drone of an engine. All was silent. The wind was still, the dogs were quiet and not a single bird sang.

It was bitterly cold and Ryan quickly began to shut the windows. The sound of bells shattering the silence froze his movements. They were like the bells he'd heard in his dream. One, two, three, four....

For a split second, the sky seemed to tear apart – ripping in two like a blue canvas being slashed with a knife.

Ryan found himself staring, mesmerized, at the rip, then *through* it into the yawning blackness beyond. Then – as abruptly as it had opened – so the sky closed up again, like an instantly healed wound. In the distance, bells continued to chime. Six, seven...

Ryan went hurtling down the stairs and collided with his uncle at the bottom. "Uncle Karl –" he blurted.

"In a minute, Ryan," said his uncle. "Things are worse than I thought."

"But the sky!" Ryan panted.

"I know, it's clear again," said Uncle Karl. "But the snow's a nightmare. It's drifted up to the rooftops in some places and not even the snow clearing equipment can get through."

"But –"

"The telephone lines are down, the mobile's still not working, and even the computer's on the blink," his uncle went on, steering Ryan into the kitchen. "We're cut off. The whole of Oberdorf is cut off."

Aunt Ingrid looked up from the table as they entered the room. "Good morning, Ryan," she said with a tired smile. "Did you sleep well? Sit down. Sit down."

Laid out on the table in front of him was salami, ham, cheese, bread rolls, coffee and orange juice.

Despite the fire, he felt cold and shivery.

Ryan was beginning to wonder whether he'd imagined what he'd just seen in the sky – whether his mind had been playing tricks after his nightmare – or perhaps it had something to do with this crazy weather. He felt calmer with his aunt and uncle around him, not that what they were discussing was good news.

"I wonder how the people farther up the mountain are coping, Karl?" said Aunt Ingrid. "If the snow's this deep down here, I dread to think what it must be like for them."

"We'll have to find out," said Uncle Karl grimly.

"Isn't there anything about it on the radio or television?" asked Ryan.

"Who knows?" said his uncle. "They're as dead as everything else. I guess it's some kind of climatic interference." He shook his head. "I've never known anything like it."

"I don't like it, Karl," said Aunt Ingrid.

Uncle Karl saw the worried look on Ryan's face and gave a broad grin. "Well, we'll just have to do the best we can, because there's no escape for the time being!" he said, giving Ryan a friendly squeeze of the shoulders. "Now eat up. If you're anything like your dad was at your age, you'll polish this off in no time."

But Ryan's mind wasn't on breakfast. No escape, his uncle had said. His whole nightmare had been about trying to escape... and failing, time after time.

No escape. Those were the very words spoken by that strange, unearthly voice with the power to vibrate the black marble walls that entombed him. *No escape.* The words that had haunted his sleep.

Pull yourself together, thought Ryan, taking a swig of orange juice. It was only a stupid dream. There were some far more important things to be thinking about.

"We need a plan of action," his uncle was saying. "For a start, there's that package for Marta." He nodded over to a brown paper parcel lying in the corner of the room. "It's marked *urgent*," he explained. "Anyway, we ought to make sure that she's okay. If you could deliver it, Ingrid, I'll go and make sure that old Geisselhardt and his wife are all right. Take Max with you."

Aunt Ingrid nodded. "I'll heat up some soup," she said. "You know how much she loves my –"

At that moment, there was a loud knock at the front door. Uncle Karl went to answer it.

"Daniel!" he said to a small man wearing a huge hat with ear muffs and an old coat. The coat was buttoned up to the neck and appeared to be straining at every seam from the quantities of sweaters underneath. "What's the latest?"

"Bad news, I'm afraid," said the man. "It's the Stock family. Hans is away on business, Eva's about to have her baby and there's no way of getting her

26

down to the hospital in Steinfeld or of getting the doctor to her."

"We'll have to get over to her at once," said Aunt Ingrid.

Uncle Karl agreed. "Tell them we're on our way, Daniel," he said. The man nodded and left.

In the flurry of activity that followed, Ryan was all but forgotten. When the time came for them to leave, Uncle Karl turned to him.

"I'm sorry, Ryan. I think you'd better stay here," he said. "The conditions out there are treacherous. Your parents wouldn't thank us if we sent you home with frostbite."

"I understand," sighed Ryan, trying not to look disappointed. He'd have liked to have been a part of the action. And what on earth would he do all by himself in the house?

"We'll leave you Max for company," his uncle added. Ryan wasn't sure that was such a good idea, but he didn't feel he could say so. He just hoped the dog would behave without his master and mistress around.

Uncle Karl opened the front door. "Good luck," said Ryan. Yet, as he watched them setting off across the featureless white landscape in their bright red padded jackets, he felt a tight knot in his stomach. He hoped they'd be okay.

With nowhere to go, Ryan took the opportunity to explore the house. It didn't take long. Although there were lots of rooms, several were empty.

The room next to his attic bedroom contained a computer. Ryan looked at it and whistled. It was fantastic: huge screen, scanner, laser printer, CD-ROM, modem... It looked as though it should be able to do anything. He sat down at the desk and switched it on.

The computer coughed and whirred, and a blizzard of snowy interference filled the screen. Uncle Karl was right. It did seem to be on the blink. Ryan turned it off again, but the screen stayed on... and the snowy interference began to form shapes. Ryan watched with fascination.

First a semicircle appeared, then a circle – and another circle. Finally, a jagged line zigzagged its way across the screen. Ryan gasped. It was forming *letters*. They were crude, but there was no doubt what they were spelling out:

DOOM

Ryan felt very uneasy. Even his uncle wouldn't be able to blame *this* on 'climatic conditions'. Could there be more unusual things happening in Oberdorf than just a freak blizzard?

Back downstairs, the brown paper package in the corner of the kitchen caught his eye. *Urgent* his Uncle had said. He went across and took a closer look. The parcel was tied up with string and addressed to:

> Fr. M. Martine,
> Das Blockhaus,
> Dunkelwald,
> Oberdorf.

'Fräu M. Martine, The Log Cabin, Dark Wood, Oberdorf,' Ryan translated. It dawned on him that *he* could deliver the package. After all, it did say it was urgent and he could easily find where to go from a map, couldn't he? Anyway, it sounded like Uncle Karl and Aunt Ingrid would be gone for ages – he'd be back well before them.

After some searching, he found a map in a kitchen drawer – together with a compass, a flashlight and a Swiss Army knife.

He lay the map out on the kitchen table, and saw that the *Blockhaus* had been marked in pen. It was in the forest just north of the village and – if the map was right – there was a track just behind the house which would lead him directly to it.

Perfect, Ryan thought. It was on a path so he shouldn't get lost and, with any luck, the snow wouldn't be so thick in the forest, under the cover of the pine trees.

"Anyway," he said to himself. "I'll have Max with me. Everything will be fine."

6

Into the forest

Ten minutes later Ryan was ready to go. He left a scribbled note on the table to say where he had gone, just in case, and stuffed the parcel into his slightly chewed backpack. With fumbling fingers, he clipped the leash on Max's collar. Taking a last gulp of warm air he opened the back door.

Outside, the snow had drifted into huge piles beside the house. He could see tracks, probably made by his aunt or uncle... deep holes in the thick, white snow. It was numbingly cold.

"We're going to Marta Martine's house," he said to the dog. "It could be a matter of life and dea–"

The moment Max heard the woman's name, the

dog pulled the leash from Ryan's hand, jumped into the snow and disappeared up to his neck. Ryan smiled and gingerly stepped out after him. The snow went up to his thighs. It was slow work covering the short distance to the forest edge.

Just as he'd hoped, the snow on the ground wasn't nearly as deep in the forest – just up to his ankles and fairly easy to walk through. What he hadn't counted on was just how steep the track was. With Max bounding along in front of him, he was soon short of breath.

"Heel, boy," he shouted, and remembered how disobedient the dog had been at the station. This time, though, Max did as he was told. Ryan grabbed the leash and Max trotted along at his side.

"Good dog," he said, and cautiously stroked his head and neck. Max looked around and licked Ryan's glove.

As the pair of them went deeper into the silent forest, Ryan shuddered. The snow-covered branches of the pine trees high above his head cut out the light and cast dark shadows across the forest floor. The deeper they went, the thicker the trees grew.

Barbed thorns. Knotted roots. Everything seemed strangely familiar. The rocks, the branches, even the track itself. It was as if he'd been here before. He had. He'd been here in his nightmare.

Telling himself he was being silly, Ryan scanned

the shadows for any telltale glints of yellow eyes. Of course there weren't any wolves, not in this forest. Max was wagging his tail happily enough, so there couldn't possibly be any, but... but... Ryan began to start running again anyway.

He ran and ran. Sometimes in front. Sometimes Max overtook him. On and on they went, racing up the mountainside between the trees until finally – gasping for breath and exhausted – the pair of them emerged in a clearing.

Ryan looked up. Ahead of him stood a little log cabin nestled in the thick snow. It was like something out of a fairytale – inviting, almost beautiful, yet, for some strange reason, sinister in its forest surroundings. He was reminded of a picture in a book he'd had when he was little.

"Come on, boy," said Ryan. "Let's deliver this package."

Ryan removed the package from his backpack, and knocked lightly. The thick wooden door flew open almost at once. Ryan found himself face to face with an old woman, no bigger than himself.

"What do you want? she snapped. Her voice was harsh and rasping.

Ryan tried not to stare, but it was hard not to. The woman's hair was a mass of golden curls; her face so heavily made up that it was like looking at a mask. A very angry mask. Ryan held out the package. "This is for you," he said nervously.

The woman seized the parcel with gnarled fingers and tore at the paper. Inside was a green tin. "Excellent!" she said, with a broad smile spreading across her bright red lips. "Come in. Come in." She stepped aside to let him enter.

Ryan hung back, reluctant to step inside. "Actually, I should be getting back," he said.

"Nonsense. Come in," said the old woman, extending a bony hand and placing it on his arm. "You're not from around here are you?" she added, suspiciously. She made it sound like an accusation.

"No," he said. "I'm Ryan Schilling. I'm staying with my aunt and uncle –"

"Of course," said the woman, looking down at Max who was strangely silent at Ryan's side. "Dear Ingrid and Karl. I thought I recognized Max. You will stay won't you?"

The words were friendly enough, but the way she said them was so creepy. Or perhaps it's just the way she looks, thought Ryan. Her dark red lips and golden hair made him think of a plastic doll's head stuck onto an old crone's body. Nasty.

The dog obediently walked through the door and settled down in the outer lobby. He's obviously been here before and lived to tell the tale, thought Ryan. I'm just being stupid. He followed reluctantly and Miss Martine closed the door behind them and bolted it.

"To stop it rattling in the wind," she explained.

"Now, come and warm yourself by the fire. I'll put some water on to boil."

The little wooden house was hot and airless. It stank of stale perfume and something else... *banana skins*. The place was so jam-packed full of furniture and things, there was barely room to turn around.

The walls of the hallway were lined with framed black and white photographs, stills of characters from old movies.

As he looked more closely, Ryan realized that the beautiful woman in every photo was the same person. It was only the make-up and costumes that were different. Then he recognized the steely glint in her eyes. The pictures were all of Miss Martine – as she had been a long time ago. A very long time ago.

"Yes," came her voice from behind him. Ryan nearly jumped out of his skin. "I was once a movie star. These are some of my greatest roles." She grabbed Ryan's arm and pulled him across to a framed newspaper clipping.

'**MARTA MARTINE: 'QUEEN OF THE SCREEN' RETIRES**' the headlines announced. It was dated 17 November, 1947.

"That was me," she said with pride. "I may have kept my screen name, but my destiny lies here in the heart of the forest. All that fame and fortune is behind me now."

Ryan's eyes flitted past the framed newspaper

clipping. Suddenly, he froze.

There was one picture that was very different from all the rest. It was an old fashioned black and white print. A woodcut... a woodcut of a building that Ryan recognized at once. The square tower, the spiral staircase, the ornate carvings – pointing to the sky, like a black marble finger. It was the clock tower from his nightmare...

7

The voice

"That picture," gasped Ryan, pointing at it with a slightly unsteady finger. "Is that from one of your films?"

Marta Martine glared at him. "No," she said. "Why do you ask?"

"I don't know," Ryan hesitated.

"Yes you do. Tell me," continued the old woman. "You recognize it, don't you?"

"No," Ryan protested. "Not really. I mean, I dreamed about it. That's all."

"You dreamed of the Clock of Doom?" she asked in a curious voice.

The Clock of *Doom*? The word hit him like a

brick. It was the same word he'd seen on the screen of the switched-off computer.

Ryan stared at the ancient picture of the familiar clock tower, remembering the touch of the cool, smooth marble, recalling the steps he'd climbed... the dark passageway... the walls closing in around him.

This was stupid. It was only a dream. "Why is it called the Clock of Doom?" he asked.

"Because that's what it is. It's no ordinary clock," said Marta Martine. "It's what's on the inside that makes it so... so *special*."

"You've been inside it?" asked Ryan. He pictured the nightmare image of the cold, hard slabs all around him. No way forward. No way back. *No escape.*

"Oh no," laughed the old woman, without smiling. "No one has seen the Clock of Doom, not in hundreds of years . . . except you."

"I told you, it was just a dream," Ryan said. It was getting stuffy in the strange-smelling hallway.

"Just a dream?" Miss Martine repeated. She fixed him with her steely blue eyes. "Sometimes dreams hold more truth than you realize." She gripped his arm once more. "Come with me. You must tell me everything."

Ryan shook his head warily. "I really ought to be getting back," he said. "Aunt Ingrid will be..."

"Come!" she repeated.

Suddenly, Ryan's head began to fill with the sound of distant ticking. Soft at first, it grew louder and louder – until it was hammering deafeningly inside his head. Ryan clamped his hands to his ears.

The old woman stood back. Max whimpered.

Out of the throbbing din inside his head came a voice. *"Help me,"* it said. *"You must help me."*

The voice – an old man's voice – was weak and faltering and it was speaking *inside his mind*.

And then it was gone.

"What is it, Ryan?" demanded another voice. "What is it? Are you all right?" Then Ryan realized it was the old woman talking now and shaking him too.

"Y-Yes. I'm all right, thank you."

Miss Martine steered him into a cluttered sitting room and sat him down in a red velvet armchair. She sat opposite him, crossing her legs and clasping her leathery hands together around one knee.

"What happened just then?" she demanded.

"Nothing... I mean, I'm not sure..."

"Tell me," said Miss Martine through narrowed lips.

"I know this sounds crazy," said Ryan. "But I thought I heard a voice inside my head."

His extraordinary hostess fixed his gaze with hers. "Ryan Schilling," she said sternly. "You haven't come here to play tricks on an old lady, have you?"

"No," Ryan protested. What a stupid thought.

"I suppose you're going to tell me you've never heard the legend?" she said. "Are you trying to make a fool of me? First you claim to have dreamed of the Clock of Doom and now you talk of hearing strange voices."

"I promise you, I'd never heard of the Clock of Doom until now," said Ryan. He was wondering how he could collect Max and get out through the front door without seeming *too* rude. "I never knew it existed until I saw your picture, and *you* told me its name."

Marta Martine put her face right up to his. He could smell a mixture of perfume and the make-up caked to her leathery skin. She stared into his eyes. "I believe you," she said at last. "I knew this day would come. The day when the Clock decided to take its revenge on the people."

Ryan looked down at his feet, embarrassed by the old woman's talk. What was she ranting about now? She's nuts, he thought. Bonkers.

"The Clock of Doom is no ordinary clock," she said. "Ordinary clocks measure and record the passing of time. The Clock of Doom, on the other hand, was built for quite a different purpose." She looked away.

"Oh, really?" asked Ryan, politely. She was beginning to sound how Ryan imagined a character in one of her old films would have spoken. All 'actressy.'

Marta looked up. "The Clock was designed to *control* time."

Max whimpered in the outer lobby, and a plaintive wail reached Ryan's ears. It grew louder and louder and became a high-pitched whistle. Ryan's skin prickled.

"That'll be the kettle," said his hostess, getting to her feet. "I'll be back in a moment."

Of course, it was only a whistling kettle. What else could it have been? Ryan watched Miss Martine leave the room.

He moved closer to the fire, and looked up at a row of shelves crammed full of books of myths, fairytales and legends.

The old woman returned with a steaming mug in each hand.

"The coffee you brought me," she explained, putting one of the mugs on the arm of his chair.

"Coffee? What coffee?" asked Ryan.

"The coffee in the package," she explained.

"You mean that's all it was? I thought it was urgent –"

"You should see me without my coffee," she chuckled. She sat back down and sipped the steaming brew. "Heaven," she purred.

Ryan laughed. The spell was broken. This was no witch in the woods. This was an elderly woman who'd once been a movie star but had lost her looks and wore too much make-up. Sure, she had a strange way of talking. She was just a little batty, that was all.

"Please tell me more about the Clock of Doom," he said.

"I'll do better than that," she said. "You can read about it yourself. I always *knew* that it was more than a legend." She headed for one of the bookshelves. "It's in a book with a red cover... Aah, here we are."

Marta Martine flipped through the book and handed it to Ryan, open at a particular page.

Ryan looked down at the title. And there it was, in black and white: 'The Legend of THE CLOCK OF DOOM'. He began to read.

8

The Legend of
THE CLOCK OF DOOM

O nce upon a time, long, long ago, in the Kingdom of Alpenpfalz, there lived a sorcerer by the name of Magoria the Mathemagician. He was a great wizard with vast knowledge and mighty powers. He knew the secret of numbers, and the hidden powers of earth, air, fire and water. Heavy magic hung around him like a fog.

Like all sorcerers, Magoria had an apprentice to help him with his work. This man, named Wytchwood, came from a distant land and, though he lacked Magoria's magical powers, he had far greater wisdom than his master.

Alpenpfalz, a small but wealthy kingdom in the mountains, was ruled by a prince who built a splendid palace at Oberdorf. His desire was to fill this royal home with strange wonders that would be the envy of other kingdoms.

It was to Magoria the Mathemagician that the prince turned for help. In return, the grateful prince showered the sorcerer with anything and everything he wanted. The air around the palace was always thick with magic.

People would come from far and wide to see the latest wonders that the prince had on show: a flying machine, a floating garden, fiery balls that illuminated every room, and fountains which never stopped and never froze.

To the prince, these were simply wonders to behold. To Magoria, however, they represented the height of his magical powers and his mastery over the elements.

Then, one day, a peasant farmer brought Magoria an amazing stone which he said had fallen from the skies. This crystal, the farmer claimed, had the power to make a fir cone grow into a mighty pine tree, in the blinking of an eye.

And so it was that the mathemagician turned his attention to *time*, and things went terribly wrong.

Magoria set to work to weave a magic spell that would magnify and control the incredible properties of this crystal from the heavens. He swore his apprentice, Wytchwood, to secrecy. Even the prince didn't know what the mathemagician had in mind.

Though Wytchwood did not tell a soul, he thought Magoria's plans were dangerous and unwise.

"Should you be working with something you do not fully understand, master?" he asked.

But Magoria would have none of it. "My magic is strong enough to tame the most powerful of forces," he reasoned. "The people of Alpenpfalz live tough lives. It's their hard work which pays for the prince's fine life and, in turn, for my magical creations. Let us repay the debt we owe them by finding a way of bending the will of the crystal to relieve their misery."

Fine words, thought Wytchwood, but he suspected that his master's real motives were to prove himself the greatest sorcerer the world had ever known.

"I am going to build a clock tower – an ornate casing worthy of housing this crystal at its heart," Magoria explained. "But it will be no ordinary clock. This magical clock will enable me to control time, so the people's lengthy hours of toil will speed by in an instant, while their moments of happiness will seem to last forever. It will be my Clock of Opportunity!"

"Control time?" Wytchwood protested. "Impossible. It can't be done! Time is but a measure of whether things are past, or present or yet to come."

"How little you've learned, Wytchwood," the mathemagician scoffed. "How wrong you are. With this crystal and my strongest magic, I shall be able to make the past the present, the future the past –

whatever I want. I will be able to speed time up and slow it down."

Still Wytchwood protested at the danger of working with the unknown. The mathemagician would have none of it. "Enough!" he commanded. "*I* am the master and *you* the apprentice."

And all the while, the crystal pulsed and glowed in its lead box on the workbench beside them.

So work began. Magoria drew up plans for a marble clock tower that would house the crystal, and began weaving the magic that would control it and, therefore, time itself.

Following his master's specifications to the smallest measurement, Wytchwood organized the construction of the tall, black marble clock tower in the mountainous forest near the royal palace. The work was carried out behind a huge sheet screen so that none of the townsfolk or villagers could see what was being built.

When the appointed day finally arrived, the population of Oberdorf had swelled to ten times its usual number. People had come from far and wide, from villages and towns and other kingdoms, to witness the unveiling of the mysterious object. In pride of place, at the very front, sat the prince and his new bride.

Magoria stood before his creation, looked up and raised his hands high. "I give you, the Clock of Opportunity," he cried.

At this prearranged signal, Wytchwood pulled a rope and the white silken sheet, taller than the highest sail, fluttered to the ground.

Everyone gasped as the magnificent clock tower was revealed, towering above the trees around it. It appeared to be pointing to the sky like a black marble finger.

They all admired the intricate stonework of the spiral staircase, they wondered at the ornate carving of the tower, and were bedazzled by the beautiful clock faces. But what was it for? Where was the magic?

"What you see is merely the outer shell," the mighty mathemagician cried. "The true wonder lies within its heart, which shall control time at *my* bidding. Winters will be short, and summers long. Bad times will become a thing of the past. From this moment forth I shall see to it that only good times prevail."

As a cheer echoed around the trees, Magoria swept around, gown flapping, and placed the palm of his hand against a raised square of marble on the side of the tower... and nothing happened.

Then, all at once, sparks flew and the air crackled with the sound of magic. A look of confusion and horror passed over Magoria's face and he was thrown backward.

DONG! The bell tolled. Deafeningly loud. The horses of the prince's carriage flattened their ears in panic and reared up on their hind legs. DONG! The people clung to one another in fear.

DONG!

Beneath this sound, another one was forming. Deep and throaty, it sounded like a chuckle rising in the throat of some giant beast... but no ordinary beast.

Something was wrong. That much was clear to everyone. No matter how many times Magoria pressed his hand to the marble, the Clock would not do his bidding.

"What's going on?" the prince called out.

The question was answered not by Magoria, but by a booming voice which came from within the clock itself.

"I AM GOING ON," it roared. "FOR I CONTROL THE CYCLE OF THE SEASONS: THE TIMING OF THE TIDES: THE WAXING, WANING MOON ABOVE AND THE MOVEMENT OF THE SUN..."

The clock was *speaking*. It had a voice. Surely even Magoria's greatest magic could not achieve such a thing? And what a voice, unlike any other heard upon this Earth. Terrifying yet hypnotic. The crowd hung onto its every word.

The mathemagician fell to his knees and hammered desperately on the side of the clock. "Stop it, stop it!" he cried – but in vain. The Clock would not be stopped.

"PITIFUL FOOLS," it bellowed. "DID YOU REALLY HOPE TO CONTROL ME? FOR I NOW CONTROL TIME ITSELF, AND THUS THE GAMES WE PLAY."

"Magoria, explain yourself!" the prince shouted above the noise. "How does this machine come to *speak*? Explain!"

"THIS PUNY MAN DID NOT CREATE ME," the Clock continued. "HE IMPRISONED ME WITHIN THIS MARBLE TOMB, BUT HIS MAGIC AND MATHEMATICS AND MACHINERY HAVE MAGNIFIED MY POWERS. SPEECH IS BUT CHILD'S PLAY COMPARED TO WHAT ELSE I CAN DO..."

And as it spoke, an icy blizzard began to blow. Whistling through the trees and howling around the tower, covering everything in its path in a thick layer of pure white snow.

Magoria turned to the prince. His face was ghostly pale. "Believe me, your highness," he cried out. "This is not what I intended."

"WHAT YOU INTENDED?" the Clock boomed. "IT IS WHAT I INTEND THAT MATTERS NOW."

The gathering of people cowered in fear, and rightly so, for this magical Clock or, perhaps the crystal from the skies at its very heart, passed judgement on all those assembled there.

"YOU, MAGORIA," it began. "THE WORM WHO DARED TO HARNESS ME, SHALL BE PUNISHED FOR YOUR INTERFERENCE IN MATTERS YOU DO NOT UNDERSTAND. FOR THIS, I CONDEMN YOU TO LIVE FOREVER AND EVER AND EVER..."

A gasp went up from the crowd. Living forever was a punishment? Magoria raised his eyes in surprise.

It seemed to him more like a reward.

"YOU, WYTCHWOOD," the clock went on in its unearthly tone, "SAW THE ERROR OF YOUR MASTER'S WAYS FROM THE BEGINNING. IF YOU LEAVE THE KINGDOM, NEVER TO RETURN, I WILL SEE NO HARM BEFALLS YOU. BUT IF YOU, OR ANY OF YOUR KIN SET FOOT HERE AGAIN, YOU WILL SUFFER THE SAME FATE AS THE REST OF THOSE GATHERED HERE TODAY."

There was an eerie silence as the crowd waited to hear their fate. They didn't have to wait long.

"HOW DARE ALL OF YOU THINK THAT I COULD BE CONTROLLED FOR *YOUR* PLEASURE. I BRING YOU THE GREATEST PUNISHMENT OF ALL – A WORLD WHERE TIME RUNS WILD, AT MY BIDDING. BUT WHEN WILL THIS FATE BEFALL YOU?" the Clock's voice bellowed. "MAYBE IN AN HOUR FROM NOW, MAYBE A WEEK, MAYBE A THOUSAND YEARS. YOU WILL LIVE EVERY WAKING MOMENT IN THE FEAR THAT IT COULD BE THE LAST BEFORE YOU FEEL MY WRATH... THE LAST BEFORE THE DAY OF DOOM ARRIVES," it roared, and the forest echoed with the cacophonous cackle of its unearthly laughter.

As the Clock fell silent, an eerie hush descended over the forest. The next moment a man's voice cried out from the back of the crowd.

"What have you done to us, Magoria?"

"Why do you get to live forever, while the rest of us live in fear?" shouted someone else.

"Our lives are ruined thanks to you!" yelled a third.

"The Clock of Opportunity?" cried the prince himself. "What you've built is the Clock of Doom!"

And as they shouted and bemoaned their fate, an extraordinary scene unfolded before them. The trees around the Clock of Doom began to grow. Creepers and vines snaked out of the ground as though they were live animals, and great bushes of thorns sprang out of nowhere. Was this a taste of what was to come?

By the time the terrified people had run down the mountainside, the clock tower was completely covered by the forest. Not even its uppermost tip could be seen above the trees.

When the prince reached the palace gates with his terrified bride, he watched in horror as the magnificent building disappeared before their eyes. It had aged a million years in one millionth of a second and crumbled away to dust.

As for wise Wytchwood, he fled the kingdom, never to return.

But what of Magoria the Mathemagician? He still lives. Even his strongest magic could not break the curse put upon him by the Clock of Doom. He is living out his sentence of a life without end, hidden in his secret chamber; and will be a hundred years hence, or even a thousand. For, remember, mankind is a slave to time, not time to mankind.

9

Trapped

Ryan closed the book and stared down at the cover. The gold letters announced:

LOCAL MYTHS & LEGENDS

He looked up to find Marta Martine staring at him intently. "Well?" she said.

Ryan shrugged. "It's just a story. A fairytale about a speaking clock," he said, trying to laugh it off. "The only speaking clock I'm ever likely to hear is over the telephone." He smiled again.

"Oh, is that all," said the old woman, with a pained expression on her extraordinary face. "You dream of a clock tower so clearly that you recognize it from the woodcut. The clock in your dream speaks which, you've just admitted, is an unusual occurrence... "

"Yes... well...er..," Suddenly an idea struck Ryan. "I can explain that," he said.

"How?"

"My dad comes from Oberdorf. He grew up here," said Ryan. "He must have told me the legend years ago. Then coming here has jogged my memory. Made me dream about it."

"And how can you explain the voice inside your head?"

"I don't know," Ryan admitted.

The old woman rose from her chair. "I gave up my career to devote my life to the study of folklore and legends of this forest and I tell you, Ryan Schilling, the Clock of Doom is not just a tale, it exists."

"Okay," said Ryan, who'd had a thought. "So if this legend *is true*, the Clock's curse came to nothing. I don't see anyone living in fear of the Clock around here nowadays. Do you?"

"But people forget, Ryan. That's something the Clock didn't think of. It misjudged the length of people's memories," sighed Miss Martine. "Hundreds of years may be nothing to the Clock... but to us? That's many generations."

"So where is it then, this Clock?" said Ryan.

Marta Martine breathed in sharply and walked over to the window. "It's out there somewhere," she said. "Hidden among the trees where the forest is at its thickest. Waiting. I've spent years trying to find it."

"Surely someone would have come across it by now, " Ryan reasoned. "By accident, even."

"Perhaps the Clock of Doom doesn't want to be found," said Miss Martine. "Until now."

Ryan twisted around to look at her. "What do you mean, 'until now'?" he asked. She was beginning to sound scary again. Who in their right mind would live on their own in the middle of a forest, anyway?

The old woman shrugged. Ryan felt it was time to leave. He couldn't wait to get away from the cramped wood cabin and its unusual occupant.

He stood up. "I really must go," he said. "Thank you for the coffee..."

"No. Thank *you* for the coffee," said Marta Martine with a strange smile. "I didn't mean to frighten you with all this talk," she added. "But it's best to know what you might be walking into."

"Yes," said Ryan, doubtfully. "Thanks again."

"Forewarned is forearmed," she said.

At the front door, Ryan clipped the leash back onto Max's collar, and the pair of them stepped out into the snow. He'd forgotten just how bitterly cold it was outside.

"Take care," Marta Martine called out as they set off across the thick snow in the clearing. "Keep to the track, and make sure you don't stop until you get back home."

"I will," Ryan called.

"Come and visit me again when the weather improves!" she added.

Not in a million years, thought Ryan. Miss Marta Martine was completely batty!

As he and Max made their way down through the trees, the dog started to act strangely. Every so often, he would tug Ryan to one side or the other, then stop and bare his teeth at something – or somebody – in the undergrowth. And the silence... It was eerie. The snow deadened every sound.

He looked around nervously. "Are you sure this is the right way, Max?" he said.

Max responded by howling up into the gloom of the forest canopy. The next instant, he bounded forward – off the track and into the undergrowth – pulling Ryan with him. Ryan lurched forward and, as the huge dog ran on, he needed all his strength just to keep a hold of the leash.

"Stop, Max!" he shouted, as branches and brambles scratched at his face and hands. "Heel!"

But the dog would not obey. It was as if he were responding to a stronger command, and there was nothing Ryan could do to stop him. "Please, Max, I can't go this fast!" he panted. Ryan's foot suddenly caught in a loop of gnarled root. He cried out in surprise as he found himself flying through the air. He landed on the icy ground with a heavy crash. As he did so, the dog leash was wrenched from his grasp, and Max darted off into the shadowy undergrowth.

"Come back Max!" Ryan shouted. But, finding himself free at last, the dog wasted no time in getting as far away as possible. Ryan was alone in the forest.

Shaking, Ryan struggled to his feet. He had to find a way out of the trees. I'll be all right, he thought, as long as I keep going downhill. That way, I'm bound to come to the village in the end.

This was a good theory, yet the further Ryan went, the more uncertain he became. Not only did he fail to come to a path, but the forest itself became denser than ever.

The trees were growing so close together that, now and then, Ryan had to squeeze sideways between their cold, rough trunks... Ryan stumbled through the thick undergrowth. Pine needles slashed at his face, barbed thorns snagged his clothes and twisted roots tripped him... but on he went. Ryan stopped in his tracks. Wasn't this what had happened in his nightmare?

He began to imagine seeing those savage yellow eyes everywhere he looked. What if there really *were* wolves in the forest? His heart pounded. He was furnace-hot and glacier-cold all at the same time. Sweat poured down his face and stung his eyes.

On and on he went. Time and again, the vicious thorns snagged his clothes and ropes of ivy barred his way. Until, finally – unable to go on and unable to go back – he found himself trapped in a wall of thorns.

He peered around him, helplessly. It was gloomy in the forest, and getting gloomier all the time.

Twisting his arms back awkwardly, he managed to slip them out of the shoulder straps of his backpack and pulled the bag around in front of him. Then he loosened the drawstring and rummaged inside for the flashlight.

He pointed the beam of light up at the branches, down at the ground, into surrounding bushes. Dark wing-like shadows fluttered through the air like a flurry of bats. Ryan trembled.

"I've got to get out of here," he said out loud, deliberately breaking the eerie silence with the sound of his own voice.

He struggled with all his might to break free – his gloves torn off by thorns which scratched his stinging hands. He was *really* beginning to panic now.

He wished he had never left the house...

A thorny branch had ripped into the back of his

padded jacket and no matter how hard he tried, Ryan could neither unhook himself nor take the jacket off.

If only he hadn't taken that not-so-urgent package to Marta Martine. If only Uncle Karl knew where he was. If only...

No one will ever find me here, he thought. At that moment, Ryan noticed something strange. For the most part, wherever he pointed the flashlight, the beam of light bounced off the tree trunks and away into the distance. But at one place, it was different. Just to his left, the light seemed to hit some kind of object: a shiny object, which reflected the light back into his eyes.

Cautiously, Ryan stretched out his arm and reached as far as the thorns and creepers would allow – fearful that, at any minute, a wolf might leap up and sink its fangs into his hand.

There was no wolf. Yet, when Ryan made contact with what was there, his blood turned icy in his veins.

The object was cold, hard and smooth to the touch. He knew what it must be. It felt like the black marble clock tower of his nightmare. Had he really found the Clock of Doom?

10

Black marble

Instinctively, Ryan tried to pull back. To his horror, he discovered he couldn't. Flat against the freezing cold stone, his hand had stuck solid. What was more, as he stood there – bent and shivering – Ryan realized that something even weirder was happening. The marble was beginning to vibrate.

What now? thought Ryan, tugging desperately at his hand. But he was still stuck. And all the while the vibrations were growing stronger.

No. It couldn't be possible... It was *impossible*... Okay, so there really was an old clock tower in the forest, but that didn't mean to say that any of the rest of the legend had to be true.

Suddenly, he remembered how the Clock of Doom had been activated in the story; how Magoria had *'placed the palm of his hand against a raised square of marble on the side of the tower'*. It had been the touch of the mathemagician's hand that had started up the Clock of Doom.

As he stood there, Ryan became aware of something else. There was a rumbling sound and the black marble seemed to be getting warmer.

All at once, his hand broke free from the stone. The slab of marble really was warming up. Ryan rubbed his fingers. They were wet and throbbing with cold. But at least he was free.

Around him, the talon-like thorns had unhooked themselves from his jacket. He could move again.

The next instant, Ryan's relief turned to disbelief, as he saw *how* he had been set free. A shiver of fear passed through him.

The creepers, climbers and thorny bushes were growing smaller. Ryan stared in utter amazement, as the vicious thorns retracted and the treacherous tendrils rewound, coiling their way into nothing.

Little by little, the forest floor was clearing itself of all obstacles, in a curious process of growing-in-reverse.

Looking up, Ryan realized that, for the first time since Max had abandoned him, he could see the sky. Like the bushes on the ground, the branches of the massive pine trees overhead were shrinking.

More than that, the trees themselves were growing smaller.

Ryan stood there as, little by little, the largest of the pines sank lower, while the smaller trees disappeared altogether. Completely dumbfounded, Ryan could only watch in silence as the forest slowly revealed what it had been guarding for hundreds and hundreds of years.

When the trees finally halted their mysterious vanishing act, Ryan found himself in a clearing. In front of him stood a clock tower which appeared to point to the sky like a black marble finger.

This was the clock tower from his nightmare, the clock tower in the woodcut picture hanging on the wall of the cottage in the woods. This was the black marble tower of the legend. He had found the Clock of Doom or, rather, the Clock of Doom had found him.

Now Ryan was really afraid. He felt sick. Sick with fear.

The forest clearing suddenly rang out with a tremendous cacophony of bells. Ryan clamped his hands over his ears and staggered back. Then, out of the chiming din, he heard the unearthly voice so familiar from his nightmare. Faint at first, it soon drowned out the sound of the bells themselves.

"YES IT IS I," it roared. "THE ONE THEY CALL THE CLOCK OF DOOM."

Ryan shuddered at the voice. Its extraordinary

tone made him cringe. Worse than fingernails down a blackboard, or the sound of a dentist's drill.

Ryan had to think clearly. He must. There was a logical explanation for everything. There had to be. There *had* to be.

He looked up at the tall black edifice. Its ornate decorations were as powerful as they were grotesque. High up above his head, a row of gargoyles grinned down at him maliciously.

Still looking up, Ryan walked slowly around the clock tower. Each of the four clock faces showed a different time. One o'clock, four o'clock, eight o'clock and twelve o'clock.

"TO THINK THAT FOOL MAGORIA BELIEVED HE COULD CONTROL ME," said the Clock, making Ryan jump. "WHAT FUN I'VE HAD WITH THE MEDDLESOME WRETCH! DO YOU KNOW WHO YOU ARE?" the Clock asked suddenly.

"Ryan Schilling," he muttered. Despite his fear, he felt faintly ridiculous speaking to an obelisk.

"YOU ARE THE FIRST DESCENDANT OF THE APPRENTICE, WYTCHWOOD, TO SET FOOT IN OBERDORF SINCE THE DAY HE FLED," the unearthly voice bellowed. "I SENSED YOUR ARRIVAL AS YOU CROSSED THE BORDER. NOW THE TIME APPROACHES FOR YOU TO PAY THE PRICE OF SETTING FOOT IN THIS LAND –"

"I don't know what you're talking about!" said Ryan.

"– AND AT THE SAME TIME, I'LL METE OUT THE HAVOC THAT I PROMISED THE PATHETIC CREATURES OF THIS PLACE." Once again it cackled with laughter. "HOW I WILL ENJOY THEIR JOLLY LITTLE DANCE OF CHAOS!"

That was when Ryan made a decision. And the decision was not to stick around. What frightened him most was the way that the forest had retreated from the Clock. This was too much like the legend for comfort.

Ryan was determined to put as big a distance as possible between himself and the clock tower. As he ran blindly through the forest, the Clock of Doom's wicked laughter echoed around his head, louder than ever.

11

Out of time

On and on Ryan ran, dodging this way and that
between the trees, hopping over the stepping
stones across a thawing stream, skidding around
boulders and bramble bushes. The snow was
melting all around him, dripping from branches
and turning to slush. It wasn't long before he was
panting noisily. His breath billowed from his
mouth like dragon's smoke, his blood pounded in
his ears and – despite the cold – sweat poured
down his face as he rushed awkwardly down the
tree-covered mountainside.

Got to escape, he thought, over and over. Got to
get away.

He came to a fallen tree trunk. Running too fast to stop, Ryan sprang off the slushy ground and flew over the obstacle. As he landed, his ankle went over and a searing stab of pain made him yelp in agony. But he couldn't stop. He couldn't rest for a second. He had to get away...

He came to a fallen tree trunk. Running too fast to stop, Ryan sprang off the slushy ground and flew over the obstacle. As he landed, his ankle went over and a searing stab of pain made him yelp in agony. But he couldn't stop. He couldn't rest for a second. He had to get away...

He came to a fallen tree trunk. *No!*

With supreme effort, Ryan managed to stop himself from springing over it. This wasn't right. This was the *third* time he'd come to the fallen tree trunk. Time really was playing tricks on him.

In an effort to break out of the time loop once and for all, he walked around the tree instead of going over it. Only when he was on the other side, did he start running again.

Once more, he was racing over the bouncy mattress of pine needles. Dodging obstacles, leaping holes, slipping on patches of melting snow. Until suddenly, there they were! The lights of the village twinkling below him. "At last!" he shouted.

He aimed the beam of his flashlight at his watch. 5:30:10. He should be back in about ten minutes. The thought gave Ryan his second wind, as he set off down the steep snowy slope.

Farther and farther he ran, loping through the deep drifts. On and on and on. And yet, no matter how fast his legs moved, the twinkling lights never got any nearer. It was as if he was running on the spot. He glanced at his watch again.

"No-o!" he howled.

It still said 5:30. The light on the digital display was flashing on and off with the seconds, but the number itself did not change. 10, 10, 10, 10, it was blinking, over and over.

It was then that Ryan noticed the village clock was chiming the half-hour below him. The sound was echoing endlessly, *as if the Clock of Doom had frozen time itself.*

Not knowing what else to do, Ryan started running again. He could only hope that the Clock of Doom would finally tire of its games and let him go.

Suddenly, the lights disappeared. Ryan cheered! If something had changed, it meant that time was moving once more.

He ran on, trying to catch another glimpse of the town. All at once, he twisted his ankle, and sat down to rub it better. Then, fully recovered, he jumped over a fallen tree trunk and was off again. Sweat poured, blood pounded, and his breath filled the air like dragon's smoke.

He was slowly feeling fitter and fitter, as his

tiredness disappeared. Around boulders and bramble bushes he ran, across the stepping stones of a thawing stream he hopped, through the trees he dodged, that way and this.

Yet as he ran, Ryan realized that, once again, something was wrong. His heart was hammering furiously, but not with exhaustion. It was with blind terror. Something had happened; or was about to happen. He leapt down onto the ground and spun round. There in front of him, was the Clock of Doom. He was back to where he had started.

"HOW I WILL ENJOY THEIR JOLLY LITTLE DANCE OF CHAOS!" boomed its unearthly voice.

Ryan was right back where he started. Those were the last words the Clock had said to him. Time was in turmoil, but what could he do about it?

12

Magoria speaks

Something was different. The *atmosphere* had changed. Although it was still dark and gloomy, there was nothing threatening any more. As abruptly as the evil power of the Clock of Doom had started up, so it seemed to have vanished.

Ryan felt a flood of relief. "It's just black marble," he muttered.

Ryan's head was suddenly filled with the sound of a voice.

"*I wish it were!*" it said.

Ryan froze. The hairs on the back of his neck stood up in alarm.

"*I wish it were!*" the voice repeated. Someone or

something was inside his mind.

"Who are you?" Ryan demanded.

"*I am the fool who brought the curse upon this place,*" said the voice, and gave a wheezy cough.

"What's happening to me?" Ryan shouted. "Am I going crazy?"

"*No, Ryan Schilling.*" said the voice. "*It's time you heard the truth. I am Magoria the Mathemagician.*"

Ryan laughed nervously. "Magoria? He's just a wizard in a local legend..."

"*Like the Clock of Doom and the tricks it plays with time, I am a reality,*"

This couldn't be happening. It just couldn't be. "You'd be hundreds of years old," Ryan protested.

"*You know the legend, Ryan Schilling. I am condemned to live forever and ever and ever. Once I was Magoria the Mathemagician, now Magoria the Moribund would be more accurate.*"

"Moribund?" said Ryan, and chewed nervously into his lower lip. He was having a conversation with someone who spoke inside his mind. This was incredible.

"*It means that I am dying, as we all are,*" Magoria explained in his quavering voice. "*Yet for me, death itself remains tantalizingly out of reach. I grow older and older and older, but cannot die. For that is what eternity on Earth must be, Ryan – everlasting old age,*" he sighed, and Ryan heard the desperation in the old man's voice. "*I need you to help me destroy this...*"

this monster that I have unleashed upon the world."

"Me?" said Ryan.

"Yes, you," came the reply. "Didn't you hear what the Clock told you? You are a descendant of the long-dead Wytchwood... Not a Wytchwood by name, but by blood, for there is Wytchwood blood in your mother's veins." He paused for breath. "It is your being here which caused the storm, the tear in the sky, the reappearance of the Clock itself... and which has caused it to choose now to wreak havoc on the people of this land."

"How was I to know?" exclaimed Ryan. This was too much.

"Your ignorance is of no concern to the Clock of Doom," said Magoria sharply. "What is important is this. It's up to you to stop the Clock before it is too late."

"Stop it?" cried Ryan. "It's not like my alarm clock, you know. I can't just take out the batteries!"

"If you fail, the tricks it has already played on you will seem like mere games."

"But I..." Ryan began.

"A lifetime of joy will speed past in an instant," Magoria went on. "A moment's pain will become an eternity of suffering. The Clock of Doom shall reign over chaos, confusion and destruction."

"You created it," Ryan said angrily.

"No. Wytchwood was right, Ryan. What I created was the clock tower and a way of magnifying the power of the crystal – but the crystal itself was not of my making. It fell from the sky. It was from another place beyond our world. How dare I think I could control something which I could never fully understand? But I have paid the price for that terrible mistake, believe me," said Magoria.

Ryan remained silent.

"But if you will not help destroy it for my sake, Ryan, then think of the others in the village and the town below," Magoria reasoned. "Think of your Uncle Karl and Aunt Ingrid. All will perish if you turn away."

"Everyone except you," said Ryan.

"If you succeed, however," came Magoria's weary voice, "the curse will be removed from the land and I will finally be released from this never-ending torment. Come and talk to me face to face, Ryan Schilling. Let us talk in person."

"But where are you?" Ryan asked reluctantly.

"Where I always am," Magoria groaned. "Imprisoned in my secret chamber underneath the old royal hunting lodge."

"Hunting lodge?" said Ryan. "Where's that?"

"Long gone, I'm afraid..."

"So what are you underneath now?" Ryan interrupted.

"The ground," the old man wheezed.

"Then how will I find you?" asked Ryan.

There was a pause. For a moment, Ryan thought the mathemagician had gone. Then he heard him speak. "There is a way," he said falteringly. "The entrance to my underground chamber lies..." The voice stopped.

"Magoria? Magoria?" Ryan called.

"... *lies where the Clock points at nine. Come as soon... as soon as you can, Ryan,*" said the sorcerer, his voice growing weaker still, "*So that we may put an end to the hideous curse of the Clock of Doom once and for all.*"

Ryan was confused. "Where the Clock points at nine?" he said. "What does that mean?"

But if he knew, then Magoria was no longer able to say. His voice had all but given up on him. "*No more,*" it whispered croakily, and faded away into nothing.

13

A race against time

Cold and frightened, Ryan stood in the forest clearing, the clock tower looming up before him... trying to make sense of what Magoria had said.

Where the Clock points at nine. What did it mean? None of the hands on the clock tower showed nine o'clock, so that was no help. So what should he do?

Ryan wasn't much good at puzzles, and that was what this was beginning to feel like. *Where the Clock points at nine.* It was a direction. It was supposed to be telling him where to go.

Clocks don't give directions, thought Ryan. But

compasses do! He pulled out the compass from his backpack. It looked just like a clock face. North was straight ahead, where twelve o'clock should be. South was at six o'clock, east was at three o'clock... and west was at *nine* o'clock.

Trust an old sorcerer to speak in riddles. Why couldn't he have simply said, 'go west'? Ryan wanted to check that he'd understood the instructions correctly but, though he called his name, Magoria's voice did not return.

Ryan set out west in a straight line from the clock tower. It was easy enough to keep on course in the newly created clearing, but harder once he entered the forest. He had to keep an eye on the compass as he weaved his way through the trees.

As he stumbled in a westerly direction, there was no sign of the remains of a building. In time, the forest began to thin and the snow on the ground grew thicker.

Then, as twilight turned to night, Ryan caught a glimpse of the moon through the treetops. He found himself thinking about Uncle Karl and Aunt Ingrid. They'd be worried sick about him, but he had more important things to think about right now. Things he wouldn't have dreamed possible.

It was getting colder. Ryan wrapped his coat tightly around him, and pulled his collar up against the icy wind.

The snow, which earlier had started to melt on

the surface, had frozen over. And with each step he took, Ryan's boots crunched through the thin crust.

He was tired and hungry, and the coldness ached in his bones. Above his head, an owl glided through the air on silent wings. Ryan looked down at the compass.

"No!" he gasped in horror. He was heading *due north*. How long had he been going in the wrong direction? When did he last check the compass?

"Where am I?" he cried. His voice echoed away, unanswered. He glanced at his watch. By a cruel twist of fate, it was actually nine o'clock.

Ryan had never felt more alone in his life... and he knew he could never survive a night in the forest.

Lifting his head wearily, he pointed the flashlight up ahead. At first, he couldn't believe his eyes. He loped forward a few paces and looked again. Yes! There was something there. It looked like a chimney.

Suddenly, with a last burst of energy, Ryan struggled down the snowy hillside at the edge of the forest. A roof came into view, and then log walls with small windows. The next minute he found himself standing in front of a log cabin. He may not have found the remains of the old hunting lodge, but at least he'd found shelter.

Ryan clomped up the stairs, across the veranda

and knocked at the door. There was no answer. He knocked again and put his ear against the wood to listen. Still nothing.

With his heart in his mouth, he lifted the latch and pushed. The door was not locked.

"Hello?" Ryan called out into the darkness.

There was no answer. He walked inside, shut the door behind him and lit up the empty room with his flashlight. Slipping off his backpack, he slumped to the floor exhausted.

*

Ryan woke with a start as the bright, early-morning sunlight streamed into the room. He sat up wondering, for a moment, where he was. Then he remembered.

He couldn't believe that he'd actually fallen asleep. Then a creeping fear entered his thoughts. Had the Clock of Doom been playing tricks with time again? Just how long *had* he been sleeping? He had to get a move on... but pangs of hunger made him think of food. He was starving.

Searching some cupboards, he found a few stale crackers and some jam which he spread on them with a finger. He washed down the 'meal' with a mouthful of snow.

Ryan crossed the room and stepped out onto the veranda. The sun was still low in the sky, and he had to shield his eyes as he surveyed the snowy winter scene.

He saw his footprints leading back up the hill. He saw the forest in the distance – and could clearly see the sinister Clock of Doom, standing tall above the trees, silhouetted against the sky. It was casting a long, thin shadow which fingered its way across the snow-covered land.

"Of course!" Ryan exclaimed, and shook his head. "I've been such an idiot."

If Magoria had wanted him to go west he'd have said so – nothing simpler. But he hadn't. *'The entrance to my underground chambers lies where the Clock points at nine'*. That's what he said. Points!

Magoria hadn't meant the time on a clock face at all! He'd been talking about the time on a *sundial* – a shadow clock – and in the middle of that sundial was the Clock of Doom itself.

Ryan squinted back across the slopes. From where he was standing, he could not see where the shadow came to an end – but he knew it was a long way off. If he was right, at nine o'clock precisely it would be pointing at the entrance to Magoria's underground chamber. Of course! The old wizard must have meant nine in the *morning* – there'd be no shadow in the dark! He checked his watch.

There's still time, thought Ryan, with a fresh surge of hope. I still have a chance, so long as I don't blow it. He hurried back inside for his backpack.

At seven fifty-nine, Ryan was ready to go. At eight o'clock on the dot, he set out into the thick, treacherous snow. He had exactly one hour to reach the end of the shadow.

Slipping, sliding, stumbling; every step was a nightmare. Time and again, he looked up at the Clock of Doom, black against the sun.

Time and again, he checked its dark shadow. Yet no matter how far he ran, it never seemed to come any closer.

I'll never make it, Ryan thought. No. I've *got* to make it! But what if the Clock plays around with time again? Don't think about it, he told himself. Just keep moving.

With his lungs aching and his heart pounding fit to burst, Ryan tramped on as fast as he could. Valuable seconds passed, minutes passed. Time was ticking away...

...Only ten minutes to go. Suddenly, without any warning, the ground disappeared in front of him. He lost his footing and rolled, head over heels, down a steep bank – and onto a track.

Ryan picked himself up. On he ran until, there in front of him, a thick black line lay across his path. The next moment, he was standing in the middle of the shadow of the Clock of Doom itself.

Would the Clock react to his being there? Would

it stop Ryan from reaching the spot where the shadow fell? There was only one way to find out.

He scrabbled up the bank and glanced at his watch again. Time had almost run out. Trying hard to keep to the firmer snow, Ryan picked his way along the length of the dark shadow, toward its tip.

He reached the end with moments to spare. At nine o'clock precisely, the tip of the clock tower's shadow nudged a half-covered rock directly in front of him.

Slowly, anxiously, Ryan pulled away piles of dead branches from the rock. It turned out to be part of a stone wall. He looked behind it and found himself staring into the shadows of a deep hole. He directed his flashlight into the darkness. Stone stairs led down under the ground.

"Yes!" he shrieked, and his triumphant cry echoed through the forest.

14

Going underground

Swiping at thick nets of dusty cobwebs, Ryan began the long descent down the damp, snow-speckled staircase. At the bottom, he found himself in a narrow stone corridor. He walked along it, shivering nervously in the cold, dank air. At the end, he came to a door.

Grasping the heavy iron handle, Ryan turned it and put his shoulder to the heavy wood. The rusty hinges creaked as the door swung open. Ryan cautiously slipped in and waved his flashlight around.

He groaned. Surely this wasn't Magoria's secret chamber at all? It looked like a wine cellar – a huge wine cellar, with a vaulted ceiling, thick pillars and row upon row of gigantic wooden barrels lying on their sides, like a row of gypsy caravans. But there was no sign of Magoria.

Something told Ryan that only a prince would have such a grand cellar, which meant that this had to be the royal hunting lodge. So where was Magoria?

"Magoria," he called out. His voice echoed around the empty vault and faded away, unanswered. He called again. Still nothing.

Ryan shone his flashlight around the cellar. The ancient sorcerer had to be in here somewhere. As the beam of light fanned out onto the fronts of the huge casks, something glinted from each of them. Ryan went to take a closer look at one of the barrels.

There, screwed to the round upturned end of the wine barrel, was a brass plate with a name and number on it.

"*Hallenfeld: 118*," Ryan read out loud, and shrugged. The name meant nothing to him. Walking on farther, he spotted a name that seemed more familiar: *Waldburg,* followed shortly after by *Steinfeld*. Of course, these were the names of the places he'd passed on the journey to Oberdorf.

But the name on the next barrel was new to him. It read: *Hexenmeisterbräu*. Ryan grinned.

"Wizard's brew," he translated. Beneath the name, instead of a number, there was a looping symbol that looked like a long flattened figure 8 lying on its side.

This was the symbol used by scientists to stand for *infinity*. Forever and ever and ever – just like the punishment given to the mathemagician. Very clever, thought Ryan. Was this his hiding place?

"Magoria!" he shouted, and hammered on the end of the barrel with his fist. "Are you in there?"

Ryan pointed the beam of his flashlight at the front edge of the barrel. If this was the right place, then there should be... a pair of hinges, which meant that on the *opposite* edge... "Yes!" said Ryan as his feverish fumblings were rewarded.

There was a loud 'click' as a catch unlocked, and the circular front of the barrel swung open. Ryan found himself staring into a gaping black hole.

"Magoria?" he repeated, more quietly this time. Silence.

For a moment, Ryan hesitated. What next? Come on, he thought, as he climbed up onto the rim. I can't back out now.

He stepped into the barrel and took a few nervous paces forward... then a few more, and a few more.

The round door behind him slammed shut with a tremendous 'BANG'.

Ryan jumped. The flashlight slipped from his hand and crashed to the floor. The light went out.

15

From bad to worse

Ryan stood inside the pitch-black barrel. This was no secret chamber. What if this whole thing had been a trap? "Magoria!" he yelled. Again, there was no reply.

Wobbly and awkward on the curved floor, it was all Ryan could do to remain upright.

Suddenly, from behind him, Ryan heard a sound that turned his stomach and made his flesh crawl... It was the sound of tiny claws scratching at the wood. *Rats*.

His mind was filled with images of twitchy pink noses, sharp claws and vicious yellow teeth.

There it was again: 'scratch, scratch, scratch',

followed by a high-pitched shriek echoing around and around the barrel. To his horror, Ryan realized that it was *him*! He was screaming.

The next instant, a crack of light appeared at the far end. Ryan held his breath.

A door was opening and then, silhouetted against a pale green glow beyond, he could see a tall, long-haired figure in a flowing dark robe.

Ryan stepped forward wincing at the brightness. "Magoria?" he said uncertainly. The figure before him wasn't at all what he'd expected. He was much younger.

"Indeed, I am," the man replied. Ryan paused. The voice was no longer old and frail. "Come in, Ryan Schilling," he said, beckoning impatiently.

The underground chamber took Ryan's breath away. Flaming torches burned brightly in every nook and cranny. The walls were lined with long, heavy wooden tables, each one covered with the instruments of the sorcerer's craft – a huge brass model of the planets rotating around the sun, a pendulum clock and some weird-looking machines.

There were bottles and pots, all marked with neat labels. There were bundles of herbs and sacks of spices. A cauldron bubbled over a low fire, sending out wisps of steam.

At the far end, in an alcove in the stonework, a single flame flickered. It burned a deep emerald green that glowed on the surrounding rock.

Then something horrible happened. Magoria – the one who had greeted Ryan, with his smooth young face, long dark hair and fine robes – kept disappearing. In his place, each time, stood a hideous figure of incredible age, with no hair, no teeth, and dressed in rags.

"What's happening?" Ryan screamed.

The ancient being raised his head, one of his milky-grey eyes turning to look at him. A gnarled and scaly hand pointed to Ryan.

"Don't be afraid Ryan... I have so little energy," the horrifying vision wheezed.

Suddenly – as if superimposed over the time-ravaged figure – the younger man reappeared. "So little energy left..." he rasped, before changing back again.

Ancient. Young. Ancient. Young. The two versions of the mathemagician flashed, faster and faster, before Ryan's eyes. He stood there, transfixed and horrified, watching the flickering blur of Magoria – both past and present.

All at once, Magoria breathed in sharply. The proud features and upright figure returned, and remained.

"Now you know what eternal life can bring," he said. "I did not intend you to see me as I really am, but... Oh, I am weary, my boy. So weary. And all this shape projection only makes me all the wearier."

"Shape projection?" said Ryan.

Magoria smiled weakly. "I wanted to look at my best when you arrived," he said. "So I conjured up the image of how I once looked. Alas, it is – as you now know – a mere illusion."

"But how?" said Ryan.

"There are many things I have taught my mind to do over the years," he explained. "As my body has grown frail, so I have developed my brain – with the aid of my sorcery, of course. How else do you imagine I knew you had returned? How else do you think I managed to talk to you inside your head and also read your thoughts? But enough of this idle chatter. There is so much we have to do if we are to put an end to the wicked curse of the Clock of Doom."

"You mean, so much *I* have to do," Ryan muttered.

Magoria looked at him sharply. "You're not thinking of giving up, are you? Can you imagine what it would be like if the Clock allowed time to run wild? Past, present and future would no longer have any meaning. Butterflies would crawl into empty cocoons and turn into caterpillars. Mountains would rise and fall in the twinkling of an eye. People would die before they have even been born... This must *never* be allowed to happen."

Ryan, who had been staring at Magoria, open-mouthed, finally found his voice. "But what on earth do you expect *me* to do?" he blurted out.

"Hush, Ryan Schilling, descendant of my wise apprentice," said the mathemagician gently. "With a clear head and a valiant heart, you *shall* succeed. But you must listen to me. And listen to me well. For one mistake, and you will surely perish."

16

The crystal heart

With Ryan looking on, Magoria busied himself around the secret chamber. First he went to a desk and removed a yellowed scroll tied up with a dusty red ribbon, and tucked it under his arm. Then he crossed to a tall bookcase, selected a large leather-bound book from the top shelf and pulled it out with a long crooked finger.

"Oh," he gasped, as the heavy book slipped from his hand and fell to the floor. He stooped down and tried in vain to pick it up. "It's no good," he rasped. "I can't..."

Ryan hurried across the room and helped Magoria to his feet. "Thank you, my boy," he said.

"And I'd be grateful if you could carry the book to the table for me." He smiled weakly.

As Ryan did as he asked, it occurred to him just how weak Magoria's body must have become. The book wasn't heavy at all. He looked back at the mathemagician, standing tall and proud in his robes.

"A mere illusion," Magoria reminded him sadly.

Ryan nodded. The image of the ancient hideous creature the sorcerer had become was still clear in his mind.

"Not a pretty sight, eh?" Magoria sighed.

Ryan turned away, embarrassed. He had forgotten that Magoria was able to read his thoughts. "I'm sorry," he mumbled.

But Magoria brushed aside his apology with a wave of his hand. "Come now," he said. "You must be prepared for every eventuality. Open the book and find me the section entitled *The Crystal Heart*."

As Ryan flicked through the book, he saw page after page filled with countless spells and detailed diagrams involving air, earth, fire and water.

"Keep going," said Magoria impatiently. "It's much farther on."

Ryan went to the end of the book, and began turning the pages from the back. There were more spells, and still more diagrams of planets and constellations, of curious machines crisscrossed with arrows and annotations... and of the Clock of

Doom itself.

Finally he came to the part Magoria had requested. In the middle of a page full of numbers and symbols was a drawing of the *crystal heart*.

"This," said Magoria, "is what gives the Clock its incredible powers. This is the crystal around which I constructed the whole clock tower. This is the heart which holds the power and makes everything possible..."

Ryan stared at the picture.

"Once you have entered the tower, Ryan, you must locate the crystal and destroy it. When you have done that, the Clock of Doom will be no more than..." he sighed, "...an over-sized ornament."

"That simple, eh?" said Ryan. "Are you trying to tell me that the crystal won't mind me smashing it to smithereens?"

"The crystal on its own has power, but not nearly the power it has as a part of the Clock," Magoria said quietly. "My magic gave it strength."

"How?" asked Ryan.

"Its position in the tower, the position of the tower itself. All these things have significance. When you weave a spell, the smallest of details is of the utmost importance."

"Okay, so it's not so strong on its own – but I still have to get into the tower in the first place," Ryan protested.

Ignoring him, Magoria went on. "The crystal is

set in a marble slab in the middle of the uppermost chamber," he said. "The rounded end sticks out above the surface. You must seize it and pull it out of its setting. But beware that your fingers do not slip. You may not have more than one opportunity to remove the crystal. Do you understand?"

Ryan nodded nervously.

"When you have removed the crystal, take care not to look at it, for it will hypnotize you with its brilliance. Instead, you must dash it against the floor, so that it breaks into a million pieces. No one else must ever be tempted into thinking that they might be able to control it."

Ryan's head was spinning. It was all down to him now. He wished that Magoria could destroy the Clock on his own.

"But I am too frail," Magoria said softly. "You know that."

"Not hundreds of years ago, you weren't," said Ryan.

Magoria sighed. "True," he said. "But the Clock has been dormant for many centuries – like a sleeping volcano – until you set foot in the land. Only now that it is active again can it be entered."

Typical, thought Ryan. It had to wait for *me* to come along. "But if it knows what I'm planning to do, surely it'll try to stop me?" he argued.

Magoria nodded. "It probably will," he agreed. "But I am here. I may be weak, but I still understand the magic of the Clock better than anyone else. I will do all I can to help you. And your greatest help is that the passage through the Clock to the crystal is an out-of-time corridor."

"A what?" asked Ryan.

"I can't explain that now. There's too little time," Magoria snapped. "When you are in this corridor, the powers of the Clock cannot affect you. Once you are inside the chamber with the crystal, however, it will be a different matter."

Magoria fell silent. As if lost in his own thoughts and recollections, he simply stared ahead.

"So I go through this passage. What next?" said Ryan finally.

"Next?" said Magoria. "Ah, yes. The ripples! The ripples!" He proceeded to break the seal of the scroll and unroll the parchment across the table. *The Ripples of Time.*

Ryan saw it was a chart. It looked like one of those diagrams which showed the orbits of the planets. Around a bright circle in the middle were seven concentric circles, one red, one orange, one yellow, one green, one blue, one indigo, and one violet.

"What are they?" asked Ryan.

"As it pulsates," Magoria explained, "the crystal sends out ripples, red or orange... all the way to violet. Each ripple is a different aspect of time – past, present, future... all you need to remember is that green is the present."

"So the others are –?"

"Dangerous? Oh yes," nodded the centuries-old sorcerer. "Wait in the out-of-time corridor until the green ripple appears. When it is shining, you must go to the marble plinth and remove the crystal. But beware. You will have but fifteen seconds to do this. If you take any longer, the ripple will change from green and your body will pass into the past or the future."

"Which?" said Ryan.

"Who knows?" Magoria confessed. "Green may be followed by yellow or blue... it may hurl you into the future or thrust you into the past... the sequence is random."

"Oh," Ryan said quietly. "Just one more question. How do I actually get *into* the clock tower. How do I reach the out-of-time corridor?"

Magoria fell silent once more. Staring into midair, his face grew troubled. He scratched his head. He rubbed his chin. All at once, the face of the hideous, ancient Magoria, reappeared, old beyond imagination, with his eyes of marble and parchment skin. Then, as Ryan continued to stare in horror, the mathemagician began to fade.

"Magoria!" he shouted. "How do I get inside the Clock of Doom? MAGORIA!"

The fast-fading shadow of a man turned his head stiffly. "Inside?" he croaked.

"Yes, inside!" Ryan said desperately. "Magoria, answer me."

For a moment, it seemed as though the ancient mathemagician was about to disappear completely. Ryan leapt forward and seized him by his shoulders.

Instantly, the figure became solid again – though still hideous.

"I must rest," he rasped wearily, and slumped to the floor. "You must press the smallest square on the upper parapet at one of the appointed times." His voice trailed away.

"The appointed times," said Ryan. "*What* appointed times?"

Magoria sighed, and coughed weakly. "The times on the faces of the clock," he said. "But... I do not remember what they are."

"But *I* do," said Ryan, with relief. "One o'clock, four o'clock, eight o'clock and twelve o'clock."

"That's it!" Magoria exclaimed, suddenly resuming his youthful appearance. "Well done, my boy! You are a credit to your ancestor, Wytchwood. It is time for you to go."

Ryan knew what he had to do, and he was afraid. It was no longer the numbing sense of unease. Now, faced with the prospect of entering the Clock, he was absolutely terrified.

"Farewell," said Magoria. "And... Oh!"

Ryan spun round. "What?" he said.

"Just a little thing I've just remembered," said Magoria, smiling sheepishly. "At the end of the out-of-time corridor is a sprung door – one that springs shut and locks when entered. It was designed for unwelcome meddlers. Even if they can get in, they certainly can't get out. Far simpler than a spell."

Ryan remembered his terror of being trapped inside the stone coffin in his nightmare. "A *little* thing!" he exclaimed.

"It's all right," Magoria assured him, and pulled a key out from the folds of his gown. "This will let you out again,"

"You're sure it'll work?" said Ryan.

"Of... of... of course, I'm..." Magoria stuttered and, once again, the upright figure of the mathemagician was replaced by his true hairless, toothless self. "It's no use," he croaked. "I cannot keep this up." He tossed the key to the floor.

"Take it and go!" he cried, and a bony yellow arm pointed to a low door in the far corner of the chamber. "It should lead you up to the surface. Farewell, Ryan Schilling," he whispered. "And may good fortune smile upon you."

17

Every second counts

Ryan finally emerged from the ground in the middle of some bushes. There was nothing to suggest that a building had once stood there.

He pushed the key that Magoria had given him into his pocket, and looked around. Far in the distance, the massive black tower stood high above the trees. He could only hope that there were no more *little things* that Magoria had forgotten to mention.

On he trudged, over fields, through woods, and back up into the forest... and suddenly he was not alone. There were hordes of people – men, women and children – approaching the clock tower. They were the last thing he had expected to see. The last person he'd seen, apart from the ancient sorcerer, was Marta Martine... and that seemed a lifetime ago.

It was horrible. The *everydayness* of it appalled Ryan. These people were flocking to look at something more dangerous than the most deadly of weapons, and they were laughing and joking about it. Didn't they realize it was evil? Of course not. How could they?

He wanted to scream out to them. He wanted to warn them what might happen. But they'd never believe him... and he had no real idea *what* might happen if time ran wild. If only they'd go away.

"Wow," said a girl looking at the clock tower up ahead. She pushed past him. "What an amazing looking thing."

"What is it? I mean, who built it?" said her friend. "And how did they do it so quickly?"

The closer Ryan got to the tower, the thicker the crowd got. More and more people were streaming up the mountain toward the curious obelisk which had so mysteriously appeared in the middle of the forest.

Then Ryan noticed that the air was growing steadily warmer – unusually quickly. Heavy loads of melting snow slipped down from the branches of the trees above, the earth turned to mud, and the forest floor was soon awash with widening streams of melting snow. Everything was happening so fast. Was the Clock still playing games?

At last – puffing and panting – Ryan emerged in the clearing directly in front of the Clock of Doom.

The whole area was thronging with excited people, all jostling for position and craning their necks for a better view. He checked his watch. It was five to one. Five minutes to go.

Ryan pushed his way purposefully through the spellbound crowd. As he squeezed between two women right at the front, he groaned.

A rope had been put up, cordoning off the area around the tower. On the other side stood a fat, green-uniformed policeman with an even fatter police dog by his side.

Ryan groaned. He had to get in there, even if it meant... Even if it meant *what*? How was he going to get past an overweight policeman and his dog? This was serious.

The people around him chattered excitedly, completely unaware of the horrors which might soon be unleashed because *he*, a descendant of Wytchwood, had returned to their country.

Darting suddenly under the rope, Ryan ran at the policeman and his dog, shouting and waving his arms wildly.

The dog barked and lunged at him. "Stay, boy!"

shouted the policeman. But, having been sitting still all morning, the dog was not about to miss the chance for some fun. As Ryan sped off around the back of the clock tower, the police dog wagged its tail and gave chase, dragging its hapless handler behind him.

Ryan glanced back as he rounded the last corner. Neither dog nor policeman were in sight. In front of him was the foot of the staircase which ran up the outside of the tower, like a helter skelter. He raced for it and – egged on by the cheering crowd who thought this was just harmless fun – bounded up the stairs, two at a time.

One flight, two flights... Six flights, seven flights... And up to the parapet. He looked at his watch again. Fifteen seconds to one o'clock –

He searched anxiously for *'the smallest square on the upper parapet'*. And there it was – waist-high and a little to the right. The countdown began.

"Ten, " he said. "Nine. Eight..."

At that moment, a heavy hand grabbed his shoulder and pulled him back. Ryan turned. It was the policeman, red-faced, sweaty and looking far from happy.

"What do you mean by breaking through the cordon?" the policeman demanded.

"I'm sorry," Ryan said, as he reached behind his back with his right arm and placed his fingers gingerly against the square. "I... errm. That is... It was for a bet," he said.

"A bet?" the policeman wheezed. "You get me chasing all the way up here... This structure could be dangerous. And look at me and not your watch when I'm talking to you."

Three. Two. One... Push!

Ryan pressed the square in the stone as hard as he could. The door in the marble slid open, and Ryan tumbled inside.

"Here, what's going o..." he heard the policeman saying.

'BANG!' The door slammed shut. At last, Ryan had made it. He was inside the Clock... The Clock of Doom.

Looking around, he saw at once how familiar it all was. The touch of the cold marble, the ornate carving of the bannister, the narrow slits in the wall which let in light. He was living his nightmare. No time to think about that. He must concentrate on the task that lay ahead.

Ryan made his way up the spiral staircase. Suddenly, he heard something that made him stop dead. A low pulsing hum was coming from the crystal, like a giant heartbeat.

With his own heart pounding, Ryan raced up to the top of the tower. Abruptly, the steps ended. In front of him was an arched doorway, and beyond that a passage. This was the out-of-time corridor. Ryan took a step forward.

The humming of the Clock stopped immediately. Ryan shuddered. There was absolute silence. Of course, having stepped out of time, he was listening to the sound of *nothing*.

18

The dance of chaos

He began to climb the steeply sloping passageway. Pale light streamed in through lancet windows which lined the outer wall. Pausing for a second to see what was going on outside, Ryan glanced out through one of the narrow openings.

What he saw made his stomach churn. He hurried to another window, and yet another. Each time he was greeted with a similar sight. Down below him, the unsuspecting sightseers were moving around jerkily and at high speed. Watching them was like watching a scene on a video tape being fast-forwarded. Then, abruptly, the movement changed, and everyone started moving in reverse.

Back and forth. Fast, slow. Fast, slow. They were seized by a time loop and spun around and around... It looked to Ryan like some weird and frightening dance. Was this the dance of chaos the Clock had threatened in the legend?

The strange effect was made all the stranger by a flashing light. On, off, on, off, it went; faster and faster. It was as if a strobe light was flashing – making the people's movements look oddly graceful as they continued to move.

Ryan looked up at the sky. The reason for the curious light show was at once clear. Night was following day at a furious rate. Time and again the bright blue sky was torn away – like a page from a calendar – to reveal the blackness of night.

But it was the looks on the people's faces that made Ryan really shudder. They were creased with pain and fear.

'*A moment's pain will become an eternity of suffering,*' was how Magoria had described their punishment. And that was exactly how it looked.

I've got to stop all this, Ryan thought, turning and hurrying along the out-of-time corridor. I must destroy the crystal. The chamber was ahead of him now. It was bathed in a deep green. Ryan bounded forward, only to arrive as the light turned to blue. He would have to wait until the green light returned.

He looked back out of the nearest window. As the nights and days continued to flash on and off, Ryan noticed that the people were getting younger. One old man threw away his walking stick and his hair turned from white to brown... He went from being stooped to upright, then shrank before Ryan's eyes until he was a baby. He was growing in reverse.

One by one, *everyone* became a baby and vanished, until the clearing was totally empty. Ryan ran to the window on the other side of the corridor. Whichever way he looked, the view was the same. The people had all gone, banished to a time before they had even been born.

Ryan couldn't tear his gaze away from the terrible sight. No! thought Ryan. This can't be happening. It can't be.

Suddenly, out of nowhere, the ground was covered in crying babies. They began to grow at different speeds, sprouting hair and getting bigger, growing up to become the people they had been before.

But it didn't stop there. Time was still moving forward at high speed.

Ryan realized to his horror that he'd been so engrossed in what was happening outside that he had missed an opportunity to step through a safe, green ripple and seize the crystal. Outside, the people were getting older still.

Idiot! he shouted to himself. Now look what I've done!

Below him, the children were racing headlong toward old age, while old people simply keeled over, one by one. Within seconds, the clearing looked like a battlefield. It was strewn with bodies, which turned to skeletons, and then to dust and blew away on the wind.

Ryan stared in horror.

He was too late.

He had failed.

The crowd, Uncle Karl, Aunt Ingrid, Max – maybe *all* the people in Oberdorf and even Steinfeld – were dead. The Clock of Doom had killed them all.

But no. Suddenly the onlookers were back. This time, marching up the hill, as they must have done earlier that day. As Ryan kept watching, more and more people threaded their way up between the trees and stood, staring up at the clock tower.

"Go away!" he screamed. "It's dangerous here!" But no one could hear him. They were doomed to relive their fatal encounter with the Clock as many times as the Clock of Doom decreed.

A police van arrived, the rope cordon was put into place, and Ryan caught sight of the fat policeman and dog taking up their positions at the bottom of the staircase. Suddenly, he saw someone else. A boy. He watched in mounting terror as the boy ducked under the rope and began leaping around like a maniac. "It's me!" he gasped, the memory of his 'living' reflection in his nightmare came flooding back to him.

Time had gone haywire. Already, the *other* Ryan was racing up the outside of the tower. Soon, he would come hurrying up the stairs.

Which is the real me? he wondered. Is that person any less *me* than I am? And what will happen if I meet myself? He didn't wait to find out.

He had to get into the chamber. He had to stop this madness. He tore back along the corridor, and was halfway through the door when he realized the ripple of light gleaming from the crystal was yellow, not green.

He pulled back at once. But it was already too late. The front half of his body which had been bathed in the warm golden light had dramatically aged.

His arms felt weak. There were brown spots of age on the back of his hands. He touched his face lightly with his fingers and recoiled at the touch of *unfamiliar skin*. It felt leathery, lined – more like the skin of a reptile than a human being.

"Oh, no," gasped Ryan, his voice strangely deep and old. "What have I done?"

Behind him, he caught a glimpse of a figure at

the far end of the corridor. It was himself. He stared back into the yellow chamber. How would the sequence continue?

If it was green, he would be able to remove the pulsing crystal once and for all. If it was something else... he might age so much he'd die.

Behind him, his double moved closer – it was about to step into the out-of-time corridor. Ryan knew he had no choice but to step into the chamber. He closed his eyes: he stepped forward.

The stone door slammed shut behind him.

19

Ripples of time

Ryan opened his eyes. There were no windows in the chamber; the only light came from the crystal itself. From the middle of a black marble plinth, at the heart of the room, it pulsed – a deep emerald green.

Ryan felt a flood of relief. That was lucky...

"*Indeed*," came the voice of Magoria in his head as he hurried across the chamber. "*Quickly, now.*" *Remove the crystal while the Clock is still wreaking havoc.*"

Ryan stretched across the marble plinth and looked down into the dome of the crystal bathed in green light. He found himself staring down at a night sky, studded with twinkling stars – a mini universe.

He wondered where this fantastic stone had originally come from. How many millions of miles had it gone before falling to Earth? It was so beautiful... so very beautiful... like a giant emerald.

"Don't look into the crystal," Magoria's furious voice exploded in his head. *"Your fifteen seconds are almost up, then the light will change from green to –"*

Ryan placed his hands on the crystal, clasped the smooth surface, tugged – and slipped.

The yellow light had left his fingers old and weak. "No," he gasped.

He tried again, and again the aged fingers lost their grip. The last remaining seconds were slipping quickly away...

"BACK AND FORTH AND BACK AGAIN," the Clock of Doom was bellowing outside. "EVERSOFAST... EVER SO SLOWWWW."

...Ryan's head pounded with anxiety as he tried, again and again, to pull the crystal from its setting. "Come out!" he muttered through gritted teeth.

"AROUND AND AROUND AND AROUND YOU GO," bellowed the Clock of Doom.

"Yes!" Ryan cried. At last, painfully, he was managing to pull the crystal from the marble.

As it gradually emerged from the hole, the crystal glittered brilliantly and, as the blue light continued to pulsate, it looked like a giant sapphire.

"*Blue* light!" Ryan gasped. "Oh no!"

The ripples of time had already changed from green to blue. Straightening up sharply, Ryan yanked the crystal from its setting and raised it above his head. Then, with all the strength he could muster, he hurled the crystal down.

"NOOOOOOOOOOO!!" screamed a voice, silenced in the second that the crystal crashed noisily against the stone floor. It exploded into a million pieces, which glowed for a moment longer – and then faded away.

"YES!" Ryan cheered into the sudden darkness.

He'd done it! He'd smashed the crystal and destroyed the Clock of Doom. But where was the door? Where was the keyhole? He looked around blindly.

If he couldn't find it then he'd be trapped. There would be no escape. Four cold, marble walls surrounded him. *No escape.* He was trapped inside the marble coffin of his nightmare.

20

Full circle

Ryan slumped down to the floor. "Magoria!" he called. Magoria?" Nothing. Where was the reassuring voice inside his head? He'd shattered the crystal. He'd broken the curse... but had he also destroyed the mathemagician? Who would help him now?

Then something began to glow in front of him. At first, he thought it was just his eyes playing tricks but, as he concentrated on the dull light, it began to shine more brightly.

Terrified that it might disappear before he reached it, Ryan hurried back across the chamber, not even daring to blink. As he got closer, he saw that the light was spilling out from some kind of hole in the wall... It was a KEYHOLE!

"Yes!" Ryan shouted ecstatically. He pulled out the key Magoria had given him, slid it into the lock and turned it. There was a soft click and the door sprung open. Ryan hurtled down the corridor.

As he ran, he noticed that his arms and hands were back to normal. How come? The blue light, he thought. This must have something to do with the blue light.

"*Exactly,*" said Magoria's voice, deep inside his head. "*The blue ripple of time.*"

"You're still alive," said Ryan quietly.

"*But fading fast, thanks to you, Ryan Schilling,*" said the weakening voice.

"Did the blue light undo the effects of the yellow light?" asked Ryan, trying to make sense of it all.

"*The yellow ripple aged your arm, and the blue ripple made it young again...*" Magoria wheezed.

"And yellow and blue make green..." said Ryan triumphantly," ...which is the present!"

"*Yes. You are as you were when you entered the clock tower. Now press the stone and leave once more. Goodbye, descendant of Wytchwood. Goodbye, Ryan Schilling.*"

With that, the voice of the ancient mathemagician faded away for the last time.

As Ryan pressed the square stone, the door flung open and shut again. He found himself standing on the parapet once more, with his back to the marble wall.

Ryan glanced at his watch. The policeman was staring down at him, red-faced and angry. "And look at me and not your watch when I'm talking to you," he was saying.

It was incredible! Not only was Ryan outside the clock tower, but he was back at the exact moment before he'd pressed the stone.

"Get back down those stairs," said the policeman gruffly. "And clear off."

Ryan turned and ran down the outer stairs. It was as though the wicked dance of chaos had never taken place – as though he had never been inside the Clock of Doom at all.

As he turned onto the final flight of steps, Ryan noticed the crowd of people grinning up at him.

"Hey, Ryan," came a voice from the back of the crowd. "Is that you? We've been so worried."

Ryan looked around. And there, waving his arms in the air, was Uncle Karl. He was standing between Aunt Ingrid and Marta Martine, with Max at his feet. Ryan bounded down the remaining steps and through the crowd to join them.

"Oh, Ryan," cried Aunt Ingrid, throwing her arms around him. "Thank heaven you're all right. Out all night in that terrible weather..."

"The forest can be a dangerous place at the best of times," said Uncle Karl. "But you look none the worse for wear." Max jumped up at Ryan and licked his hand. "We've been looking for you everywhere," his uncle added.

"When the Clock appeared I suggested that we might find you here," Marta Martine interrupted. "I explained to your aunt and uncle how good it was of you to bring me my *medication*."

"Well, yes," said Uncle Karl. "It was a kind thought, Ryan – but you really shouldn't have left the house." He slapped Ryan on the back. "The main thing is that you're in one piece, though. What a time to come to stay in Oberdorf. First the incredible snowstorm, now this strange clock tower and the sudden thaw. I've never known anything like it."

If you only knew, thought Ryan. If you only knew.

He glanced up at Marta Martine. A faint smile was playing on her bright red lips.

Ryan frowned thoughtfully. There was something he still had to do.

The next morning, having asked his uncle if it was okay to go for a little walk, Ryan set off once again in search of the site of the ancient hunting lodge.

He eventually found the concealed stairway, and followed it back down to Magoria's underground chamber. Then, with bated breath, he lifted the latch and pushed the door open.

The secret chamber was just as it had been the previous day. The flaming torches on the walls were still bright, the rows of apparatus were still in place and the cauldron was still bubbling. But the occupant of the chamber, Magoria himself, was nowhere to be seen.

Ryan called his name. Gone, he thought. Had the ancient mathemagician somehow managed to leave his underground prison? Or had he finally died at long last?

Ryan saw the book and the chart of *The Ripples of Time* lying on the table where he had left them. Beside them was something else – a letter. It read:

Thank you, Ryan Schilling,

Like Wytchwood before you, you were a true friend. With the crystal gone, thankfully, no man can live forever.

Magoria.

Ryan looked up and found himself staring into the alcove. Of course, he thought. Something *is* different. The flame. The mysterious emerald green flame. It had gone – and with it, the ancient sorcerer.

As he turned away, Ryan noticed a threadbare gown lying on the floor by his feet. He crouched down and touched it. As he did so, it – like the bones beneath it – crumbled to dust.

USBORNE SPINECHILLERS

Letters from the Grave

When a new girl at school is the victim of bullying, dark forces from the spirit world are unleashed. An invisible hand writing mysterious messages on the blackboard is just one of a horrifying chain of events that quickly spirals out of control.